GOD
WALKS MY
DREAMS

GOD
WALKS MY
DREAMS

RANJANA KAMO

PARTRIDGE
A Penguin Random House Company

To order additional copies of this book, contact
Partridge India
000 800 10062 62
www.partridgepublishing.com/india
orders.india@partridgepublishing.com

$\mathcal{A}$cknowledgements

With thanks to God for actually walking with me as I wrote this novel . . . .

With special thanks to my Mother Mrs. Raj Kamo . . . . today and forever . . . . for her constant encouragement to me that instilled confidence in me to write this book and for the precious time spent by her in going through my book with patience to do a proof reading for me.

With thanks to my Father Mr. Ramesh Chander Kamo for showering his blessings from heaven.

With thanks to my Brother Ramnik and Sister-in-law Garima for being there for me.

With love to my lovely Nephew Neel
and Nieces Ruhi and Nina.

$\mathscr{P}$reface

Life offers us many opportunities and it is up to us to accept or deny them. 'God Walks My Dreams' is the story of a man who did not lose his faith in God and chose to accept every opportunity that came his way. You need to read through to know the consequences of the choices he made.

All the characters and places as well as the incidents described in the book are imaginary and any resemblance to someone/ someplace/ something could only be a mere coincidence.

I am sure each one of us can relate to one or more characters in the story by translating their triumphs and failures to incidents in our own lives. It is always easy for us to give up in trying times but those who sail through troubled waters succeed in creating the real impact and become an inspiration for others.

The narrative of the characters in my book is based on simple observations of human behaviour which have taken the shape of an imaginary plot where I have tried to weave various pieces together to make a story. The theme for the book shaped up as I drove through the roads of my city and observed people around me. I finalized the theme when I saw the steam rise from my electric kettle as I was boiling water for our daily cup of tea, an elixir that wakes up my world for me.

We all complain of paucity of time for everything in life so I have made an effort to keep the narrative crisp and concise and the pace relatively fast for the readers to go through the entire book in a short time. It was the same paucity of time that I faced while penning down this story. It has taken me almost six months with strict time management to run my fingers on the keyboard of my laptop to get this book completed.

Let us read on and get inspired!

$\mathscr{C}$hapter 1

I did not know anyone in this city and this city did not know me. The city and I were perfect strangers for each other. I was one in the crowd with a fear of being lost in the multitude of people but I had come here with a dream in my heart, a dream to make a place for myself in this crowd of this famous city of Gaulpur.

There was a voice calling from deep within my heart that had brought me to Gaulpur, the City of My Dreams, the City where my dreams were waiting to be explored and brought to life. I wanted the sun, the moon, the stars, the planets, the sky and the entire constellation packaged into one!! I did not want to settle for anything less than that. I think it was destined in my name 'Suraj', the 'Sun', a fiery Sun that wanted to shine brightly with brilliance and be seen shining across the universe. I wanted to lead the world like the 'Sun' and have my name written on every cloud that emerged in the sky.

I knew my wishes from life were extraordinary and I was willing to give life my very best to shape them into reality and here I was in Gaulpur to make a beginning to leap into what life had in store for me and what best I could make of it. I was sure of not leaving any opportunity that I could lay my hands on to avoid having to look back in life and regret for losing out due to a small miss out. I owned nothing but my dreams were to possess everything in the world. I was like an empty bowl waiting to feel the touch of gold coins sliding in with a clang, a clang that would gradually turn into a soft musical note as the coins fill me up to the brim. I wanted to hold my life in my hands and steer it at full speed directly to my dream destination. But there are no short cuts to success in this ruthless world where survival needs an endless struggle and success requires an additional dose of good luck together with the struggle for survival and the extensive willingness to go an extra mile!! And I was ready to go an extra mile or maybe many extra miles if required. I was ready to take a plunge into the deepest ocean in search of my oyster and my pearl. I was ready indeed!!!

It is good to dream but realizing a dream means hard work and patience and a touch of good luck. I wanted an opportunity to build a base for myself in Gaulpur and make the most of it to reach the skies of my dreams. My mother's advice for taking care of my health together with my father's valuable lesson for a worthy life, "Listen to your heart but always do what your mind tells you is right," echoed in my mind as I alighted from my train from Murli, my home town.

I took a deep breath to feel the air of Gaulpur. I wanted to become a part of this air and this life. The air of Gaulpur gushed through my lungs and welcomed me by settling in every molecule of my body. I wanted to be one with Gaulpur and be called a 'Gaulpurian'. I looked at the sky and shouted, "Gaulpur, here I come!!!" The passersby looked at me with amusement and some even smiled at me. I again took a deep breath to drown myself in Gaulpur's essence. I was breathing Gaulpur!! I was breathing Gaulpur and this thought was filling my heart with great excitement and abundant happiness. The thought of being in Gaulpur itself made me feel that I had achieved half of my goal. It was a heartening experience to set my feet on the land of Gaulpur. The joy of the experience was no less than that of the first man to land on the Moon. I seemed to have accomplished a special feat. This air of Gaulpur was very different from the air of Murli. It was not as fresh as it had been in Murli due to the pollutants mingled in its freshness but I was still happy to be breathing it. It was the air to my life's gateway and I was immersing myself in it.

I had finally arrived in Gaulpur!!

I heard thunder and looked up to the skies above. Black clouds were rolling in and there were streaks of lightning in the sky welcoming me to Gaulpur!! I walked out of the railway platform and stood under the open sky as I wanted to get drenched. I stood there for long as the rain kept soaking me with all its might. I was happy and the onlookers shook their heads in disbelief. I did not care as the skies were greeting me, their own Suraj, by mingling with me through the loving embrace of their showers!! It was a hearty welcome into the city of my dreams. "They have fireworks in my honour today," I said to a man standing at a distance as I pointed to the lightning in the sky. He looked amazed, amused and confused by my remark so he just walked into a kiosk to get away from me. I am sure he thought I had been struck by insanity. But I could not care less. I was in Gaulpur and that was all that mattered to me at that historic moment of my life. I was jumping into puddles of water to make splashes all around me as I wanted Gaulpur to know that I had arrived.

I looked around the station and decided to make the railway platform as my temporary dwelling till I could find a permanent place for myself.

Chapter 2

Murli, my home town, is a small and beautiful town five hundred and two kilometers from Gaulpur with a population of about seven thousand people. Murli has a mystifying green landscape which lends a lining of pride to its overflowing beauty. *Gulmohar* trees adorn every street as they proudly stand on both sides of the road with their heads held high and branches fully laden with red and orange flowers protected by the lush green leaves keeping the roads shaded and cool even during peak summers. They shed their flowers on the roads to cover them with an amber colour carpet. A vast expanse of the land of Murli is covered with wheat and sugarcane fields. Migratory birds bring cheer to the dull weather in winters as they travel thousands of miles only to be with us at Murli. Their multiple colours bring a comforting smile on our faces and gaiety in our lives and their chirps fill the air with vibrant music. The houses are small but well contained and the people are basically happy and contended with whatever little life has to offer them. There is a small pond in the central hub of the town that is flanked by some houses on one end and the other end leads into a dense forest known for its sandalwood trees. The pond is called 'Sinda Talaab' and it houses some fish and frogs and a few ducks. There are two main markets that feed the town dwellers, one in the central hub and the other in the eastern part of the town.

The people of Murli survive primarily on farming. Each household has livestock that helps take care of the daily needs for milk, butter, *ghee* and eggs. Murli is a land of the 'lazy'; the land where the day, the afternoon, evening and night are all so lazy that I yawn each time I think about Murli. The people of Murli are laid back with very little to do apart from tilling the fields, taking care of their livestock and sleeping. The afternoon siesta begins at eleven in the morning and lasts till the evening for the elders of the town. Life for the other inhabitants of the town is 'easy go lucky'. The livestock yawns through the day and the trees sway softly and slowly for the fear that they may not wake up the town with the sound of the music of the air as it blows through their leaves. The air of Murli has a touch of laziness in it which gets into everybody's blood circulation system making them take life with the utmost ease that leads them into postponing everything to the next day without realizing that tomorrow may or may not come. Life for the town dwellers is built in tomorrow and day after, today is only for lazing out throughout the day.

The children of Murli study at the local schools and those who can afford to study further go to the college in the nearby city of Devon. Devon is a modern city that has some very reputed colleges to boast of where all possible education streams are taught to students who flock the city from various parts of the nation. I liked to walk through the main market of Devon whenever I visited the city. The shops here were of a different league as compared to the shops in Murli. They spoke of the rich class of people that inhabited Devon. Shops at Murli were just able to cater to the average class customer segment. They were stocked with the average brands and were very modestly decorated whereas the shops in Devon were flashy and flamboyant and stocked all the high end brands as the spending power of people here was on a much higher side. The two cities were on the extreme ends of the spectrum if compared for the lifestyle of their people, the cash in circulation, the density of their population and even the basic infrastructure of buildings and roads. This made Devon as the preferred place to holiday for the Murli dwellers.

I had completed my schooling two years back. My parents could not afford to send me to college so I had spent my time at Murli helping them at the fields. We grew sugarcane in our fields and supplied it to the sugar mills at Devon. We would load our ten year old rusted tractor with sugarcane and drive to Devon to sell our harvest at the auction held by the sugar mills. We had to make six trips each time to sell our entire harvest. We earned a decent amount on the harvest that helped us survive through the year. I would lend a helping hand to other farmers too and drive them to Devon for a small fee. I was working at the fields with my father but my heart lay elsewhere. I would spend the day dreaming about my future where I would come out of my palace dressed like a prince and get into a white luxury sedan driven by a driver in white attire. I was unhappy with the way things were shaping up at slow speed so I had decided to take the first step to move out of Murli to Gaulpur to find my palace and my sedan.

I had seen the landlords of my town lead a luxurious life and I wanted the same for myself. The landlords had a palatial house called 'Jalpari' near the outskirts of Murli where they lived like Kings. They had an extravagant and pompous lifestyle derived from their abundant wealth which came from their real estate business and the tea gardens owned by them in the nearby hills of Jyoshi. I aspired for a similar lifestyle each time I passed by their prosperous house. The ambience of the house and the surroundings had an aroma of wealth which you could breathe from a distance as you approached the magnificent gate to the farmhouse. Jalpari was a palatial house made of pure white marble that had green granite minarets on its four corners. There were beautiful sprawling gardens in front with sunflower beds in the middle. The approach road had palm trees swaying on its sides lending the feel of a beach to the ambience. There was a golf course at the rear end of Jalpari where the landlords played golf every morning. I had always seen Jalpari from a distance and loved the white and green combination of marble and granite that gave it the theme of a serene white lotus being guarded by lush green leaves. I had noticed some horses galloping on the side of the mansion. Jalpari had every touch of royalty that always inspired me to build a royal empire for my parents. This required me to move out of Murli and that was the genesis of my decision to move to Gaulpur. Devon could also have been a good option but I was thinking big so I chose Gaulpur instead.

My memories of Murli were fresh in my mind and each time I thought about Murli, I had flashbacks of my mother sitting near the window knitting a cardigan for me or cooking a meal for us and my father holding the plough at the fields or sitting in the verandah with his friends.

My memories would then shift to the grocery store at a distance where my friend Raja sat lazing at the cash counter. The shop was owned by Raja's father and that gave him all the liberty to visit the shop off and on and work as per his whims. I could imagine him sitting at the shop with a walkman plugged in his ears to listen to the latest movie songs. His father would lash out at him as he always remained lost in his thoughts and did not pay attention to any of his father's instructions. Raja had a clear vision for his life. Life for him meant spending some time at his father's shop and earning some money to buy movie tickets. He did not want anything else from his life. Raja and I had one thing in common, we were both sure of what we wanted in life and our goals for life were well laid out in our minds. We spent hours playing in the fields. We would swim in the Sinda Talaab, fly kites and sing songs while we chased the birds in the fields. Raja and I spent the afternoon racing with the goods train that blew its horn with all its might as it hissed through our town thrice a week. At times we would race on foot and there were times when we raced with the train on our bicycles. The dogs of Murli raced with us as we tried to outrace the train. Our faces turned black with the dust and sand and the soot but we were too carefree to bother about it. The train would not come on Wednesday, Friday, Saturday and Sunday and we spent these four afternoons throwing pebbles in the Sinda Talaab. We would either compete for making the maximum number of ripples in the water or for throwing a pebble at the farthest spot in the Sinda Talaab. There were times when we would count the ripples made by the buffaloes that were left astray to swim in the pond by their owners. Life was at its simplest realm at Murli. We had another pastime and that was stealing fruits from the nearby orchards. I was tall enough to jump and grab fruits from the trees in the orchards that fringed the town. Raja and I were fond of guavas and mangoes.

The orchards at Murli were known for their extra delicious fruits. Raja was not very tall so I had to pluck fruits for both of us. I would let him stand on my shoulders at times so that he could pluck fruits of his own choice. We were caught by the guards often but we knew how to dodge them and flee. Our evening snack was usually fruits from these orchards. It was the thrill in running from the orchards that made us steal the fruits from there.

It was difficult to transport myself back from these memories to come back to the present and it took me some time to switch off my emotions and think about my life ahead. Coming back to present day reality was tough and I could see a long road ahead to my dream destination and I did not know where to begin. I knew I would miss my parents at every step of my life and that tore me apart. I am the only son and the only child of my parents and they have showered all their love on me. I am blessed to have the best parents in the world. Leaving them was not easy as I had left a part of me with them. I had to be uprooted and cut off from my family tree to move to Gaulpur. The sacrifices my parents and I had made kept me moving ahead in the toughest of times. I would recollect about their sacrifices and their love for me each time I thought of giving up. This helped me derive the strength to move ahead in life.

$\mathscr{C}$hapter 3

Murli seemed like an infant when compared with the big brother Gaulpur. Gaulpur is a cosmopolitan city alive and buzzing with continuous activity and it hosts a population of ten million approximately. I was here to add another number to the population of the city. Gaulpur is the place to be, a very happening and amazing place. I was awe struck looking at the sky scrapers that were hugging the sky. My neck would hurt as I spent hours gazing at them. I could only see concrete till the horizon. I had never seen so many people in any festival or fair back home that I was seeing here in just one street of Gaulpur. I had found another meaning to civilization here. I felt like Columbus on a discovering spree. It was my voyage to the island of my dreams and Gaulpur was my ship that would cruise to that island for me. The city looked prettier at night with lights lining every building and corner. This is a city of festivities where I could see people busy with celebrations and parties all the time. This city does not sleep and back home at Murli all households called it a day by seven in the evening. The traffic is maddening in Gaulpur. I almost got hit couple of times during the first week of my arrival in the city. Initially it was difficult to walk on the streets with vehicles zipping through every possible inch of the road. I had never seen so many vehicles in one place till now. The roads resembled a car factory continuously releasing its inventory of cars at jet speed throughout the day. It took me some time to gain the expertise to navigate myself on the roads with speeding traffic surrounding me. Another striking feature of the city that caught my attention on landing here was the disparity in the lifestyles of its people. Gaulpur takes pride in the huge villas spread across its territory but this pride is undermined and shadowed by poor hutments that flank these rich villas. The rich and richest and the poor and poorest are living together in this city of Gaulpur. This is the irony of big cities and Gaulpur is no exception to this rule. The culture of people is also diverse as the city has migrants from different cities and states. The city has mixed the various cultures and developed a new concoction of cultures for itself, the Gaulpurian Culture. The language of the people is also a blend of the various languages that the inhabitants speak.

I was a stranger in Gaulpur, I did not know anyone here so there was no one I could ask for help or support. I had to struggle alone and find my own path. I had to design my own destiny and something told me that one day for sure I would carve it out to my desire. I would walk for hours in the meandering streets of Gaulpur looking for a place to stay and a job to last. Things were not always looking up to be at their best but I knew I was not going to give up. I had travelled far from home in search of a job and I would need to find it soon. My feet were swollen and they hurt a lot but I pushed myself to continue. I was confident that Gaulpur would not let me down if I held my head high. The city of Gaulpur is the most visited city and boasts of famous people who have made a fortune and have both national and international presence. I too wanted to be a well known figure and have a good bank balance that would suffice for a well to do lifestyle for my parents and me for the rest of our lives. The only encouragement I had was that nine out of ten successful men have humble beginnings like mine and all of them need to struggle to see their dreams come alive. I was willing to struggle and fight for my dreams and that is what had brought me to this city. I was walking the lengths and breadths of the city everyday and soon knew the street map of Gaulpur by heart. The major streets and their landmarks were stamped in my memory and I could walk up to them without getting lost even in my sleep. I seemed to have a GPS downloaded in the software of my grey cells that navigated me to any street of Gaulpur that I wanted to go to in an automated mode.

$\mathscr{C}$hapter 4

I had to find an accommodation soon but I needed a job to afford the rent. It was thirteen days since I had moved to the city. It was like an endless wait in search of the first opportunity to strike and help me build a launching pad for myself. I had to keep my patience intact and face each day with all the confidence that I could gather from within myself. I would do breathing exercises and reinforce my confidence by praying to God and giving pep talks to myself. I had become my best friend and companion while facing life in its rawest form. Life was getting tougher day by day making me emerge stronger with every hardship that I faced. I knew that I was bound to succeed if I did not give up. I was living on the railway platform and sleeping on the platform bench with my bag tucked under me. The weather was supporting me as it was pleasant and I could sleep without having to cover myself with a blanket. I was surviving on water and homemade snacks and cookies that I had brought with me from Murli and had to find a job soon and I knew jobs in big cities are hard to find. I was wishing that I could find a job before my stock of snacks vanishes from my bag. I wanted to feel the joy of replenishing the snacks with my first salary and that made me restless as I was still far from getting a job. I was tired but still very hopeful. I had little means to support myself in this magnanimous city. I would cling to my grey bag, my prime and only possession, and dreamt of owning a house of my own very soon. I had just one set of clothes in my bag in addition to the clothes I was wearing. My shoes were worn out and my socks had torn but my enthusiasm was unperturbed. I could see my toe sticking out from my torn sock and torn shoe like a toad pushing its snout out of water for a breath of fresh air. I would twiddle my toe and play peek-a-boo with it during the night while I lay on the bench under the moonlit sky. I had a wooden bench for a bed, the crescent of the moon as my night lamp, the dark night sky as my blanket and the stars to remind me that I was beginning a life in Gaulpur. I would pray to God and go to sleep counting the stars in the deep blue sky above. I was in a hurry and wanted to get a job before the crescent of the moon turned into a full circle.

Each day brought with it a new experience and a new struggle. People were not easily accessible as they did not want to waste their time in talking to a stranger. Time for businessmen means money and they did not want to waste any money in meeting an unknown beginner like me. I would still manage to meet ten to twelve people daily and ask them for vacancies in their stores or offices. It was not easy looking for a job in this big city. I daily came across many other jobless people like me walking the streets of Gaulpur in search of a job. There were times when I would lose hope and think of giving up but then use all my inner strength to revive my confidence and optimism and hold myself strongly to face the next day. I did not want to return to Murli as a loser. I wanted to go home to my parents with my head held high and have the joy of success walking proudly with me when I would cross the 'Murli Zero Mile' milestone.

Days passed by and my struggle continued. I was utilizing every opportunity to work and earn. I took up every odd job that I could lay my hands on to earn whatever little amount that was possible. There were times when I helped the vendors at the railway station deliver their snacks or other goods to customers in the trains. I had to run from the vendors' stalls to the train back and forth like an Olympic athlete. I had to deliver anything one can think of . . . . tea, coffee, juice, handkerchiefs, socks, packs of playing cards, bags of chips, candies, magazines, books, toothpaste, shaving cream, combs, etc., etc., etc. and get the cash for it from the passengers before the train moved out of the railway station. There were times when I had to jump off a moving train. The vendors paid me in kind with a bag of chips or a cup of tea or a glass of juice. It was indeed fruitful to be at the railway platform as it helped me get odd jobs to help satiate my hunger and it also provided me a shelter to sustain in the city. This was a home away from home; a shelter that helped me during my initial period of stay in the city. I would also help passengers carry their luggage whenever I was at the railway station and earn enough to buy myself a cup of tea and a bun. Some passengers would only bless me instead of tipping me for helping carry their luggage. I was happy to get their blessings as I knew that these too would surely help me at some point in my life. The other porters did not want any competition from me and this showed in their hostility towards me each time I tried to help any passenger. They would push me aside and run to the passengers as soon as any train arrived. The porters stared at me with red hostile eyes that said that they meant business and I should stay away from the passengers who they presumably laid right to as though they were their own property. I still managed to help one or two passengers and earn some money for my tea and bun. Tea and bun had become my staple diet and I named it 'Buntea' for short. My day would begin and end with a Buntea. I would sit at the tea stall and watch the stall owner Sundar make tea for his customers. The tea leaves would jump around and dance in the boiling water that bubbled in the pan on the small stove that stood on a broken red brick wall. I liked to watch the water in the pan change its colour with the tea leaves bursting open to release their colour as they swam and dived in the bubbling water in the pan. The colour of tea would change from darkest green to darkest brown to black in no time. Sundar would then add milk to the concoction and boil it till it was dark red. It was a beautiful sight to see the milk spread through the dark blackish brown water and change its colour within seconds as it totally mingled with the tea. The steam from the pan would rise and condense on the glasses of Sundar's spectacles. Sundar would continuously wipe the layer of condensation from his spectacles and mumble something to himself in his native language which I could never understand but liked to listen to. His temper matched the intensity of the boiling tea as he seemed to swear in his native tongue. I could watch the dancing bubbles in his pan all evening as I was too free to do anything else after the end of a struggle filled day. My reflection in the tea shone clearly as it rocked slowly to and fro and folded into ripples with the waves of the boiling tea. Sundar's stall was frequented by passengers in transit and porters alike. He was making tea, an elixir that instilled life into tired bodies. He was waking up the tired and sleepy world with his elixir. The railway staff at the station also came to him for their daily dose of the elixir. I often helped Sundar in serving tea and buns to his customers and got a cup of tea in return. I would wake up to the sizzling sound from his sauce pan that grew louder as he poured hot steaming tea in the cold ceramic cups. The sizzling sound and the aroma of tea were sufficient to make my sleepy eyes open wide and force me to get up early every morning. I seemed to have a strong connection with this aroma and colour of tea and life had designs to make this bond stronger with time. I would spend the wee hours of the morning sipping hot tea with a bun. The buns were really coarse and tasteless so I dunked them in my tea and swallowed them with great difficulty. The Buntea breakfast was a survival mode for me. My mother would have cried seeing me swallow a brick like bun as she had always given me the best of food that we could possibly afford. I would recollect the hope that had illuminated her face when I left home and that made me eat whatever I could get to survive to reach my goal in life. I reminded myself that I had to fulfill her dreams!! There was a glint of hope that had made her eyes sparkle as she bid me goodbye and I had to realize my dream soon to shape that hope into reality. I wanted to make her life so comfortable that she would spend all her life smiling. I had to make my parents proud and give them a lifestyle similar to the one that was led by the rich landlords of Murli. I wanted to make their life extra special.

*C*hapter 5

It was my fourteenth day in the city and I set out on my daily job hunt mission with my grey bag, a smile on my face and a confident spirit. The sun was shining bright with the day temperature fuming at its peak making the beads of perspiration run down my face and back and tickle me in the weirdest possible ways. My eyes could barely remain open with the sunshine blinding them. It seemed like the hottest day of the century with mercury rising at an unusual record breaking speed. My shirt was soaked in perspiration and my lips were dry to the extent of making their skin crack like cracked patches of mud in the land of a parched desert. My energy had been totally drained by the heat and I could barely walk. I was tanned beyond recognition and looked like a roasted cocoa bean wrapped in clothes. My once upon a time fair feet were now giving my brown shoes a competition as I could not tell which one of these was darker in colour.

I walked past the stores in the heart of the city trying to look for 'Hiring Now' signs. Every notice and each sign that my gaze fell upon seemed like a job offer to me and the sight of a sign made me rush to the store and find the store owner and convince him that I was the most suited for the job. The day was not as good as I had expected it to be. Luck was not on my side as I was greeted with negative responses throughout the day. My hope would rise like the high tide and splash on the seashore with an expectation to bring back a rock with me but each time I splashed I only touched sand that washed back with the water as it retreated to the sea. I knew that God wanted to see me struggle hard before he would grant me any wish so that I could value my success. He was going to make me wait for my special oyster that would hold a pearl in its arms. I was going with the flow of life and letting God pull at my strings and take me along the path that He had designed for me. I had full faith in Him and His decisions for me so I faced whatever life offered to me with immense confidence and optimism. I recited my prayers, the *Gayatri Mantra,* every morning before setting off for my job hunt as it boosted my confidence.

The last stop for the day was a small house at the end of 'Jogi' Street. A guard in the street had informed me that this house needed a helper. This was my last hope for the day. I would have preferred to find employment in a store or an office but here I was ready to ask for the job of a domestic help as things were not materializing as per my wishes. I was dreaming of working in the house as a helper. I had a duster thrown on my shoulder, my sleeves and the legs of my trouser rolled up. I was running around the house to broom, mop and dust the house, clean the car, wash dishes, ... whew . . . . , wash clothes, mow the grass, water the plants and chop vegetables, ... God I was so busy . . . , when I heard a crow cawing in the ugliest tone ever. I looked up and realized that I was still standing at the gate of the small house in Jogi Street. I knocked at the white door of House Number 31 on Jogi Street. I heard the door creak and a child peeped at me through the semi open door. I could only see the boy's dark brown eyes peeping curiously at me through the thin gap in the door. I had just opened my mouth to say something when a dog pounced at me. I pushed the dog away and ran for refuge. The duster disappeared from my shoulder and my sleeves were back in their place as I was brought back to reality in the crudest and cruelest possible way. I was running madly to safety. I must have run over a mile before I stopped and turned around and was relieved to see that the dog had not followed me this far. I was panting and choking as I was breathless. I had stopped running as my energy had drained out and I was so tired that I could not have put up any resistance to the dog if he had tried turning me into his lunch. I thanked my stars that the dog had not followed me. It was a tough day and a tougher mile long marathon on an empty stomach. I had no strength left in me and I felt as weak as a dried branch of a dying tree. I needed a good meal to help my intestines come back to their original shape. My stomach was hurting with continuous cramping due to starvation. I drank some water from the tap in the nearby park and collapsed on the grass feeling like a little puppet whose strings had been left loose by the puppeteer. The grass embraced me and I sank into the ground like a child hugging his mother. I closed my eyes and lay there in a subconscious state of mind. I had sunk into the wet grass and was still sinking into its muddy patches and did not even have the energy to move my hand.

I fell asleep in no time and was woken up by the chirping of some birds. Two sparrows were perched on the bark of the tree on my side and they made sure that they turn into a wake up alarm for me with a tangy shrill in their chirps. I raised my head and tried to open my eyes. It was difficult to get up as I was in deep slumber. I blinked my eyes as sleep resisted them from opening fully. I lifted myself up with great difficulty and looked around to see where I was. It took me some time to figure out why I was sleeping on the grass. Sleep and starvation had made my faculties sluggish and I was still in my dream land. I had dreamt of a monster and a dragon fighting over a deer. The deer was running for its life followed by the monster amuck in frenzy. The dragon was running berserk to catch the deer before the monster got to him. The dragon was about to pounce on the deer when the birds started to chirp and woke me up. I tried to interpret my dream and inferred that I must have been the dragon and the dog was the monster that fought with me to send me away from a new job (the deer) that could have been mine if the monster (the dog) had not decided to pounce on me. I shook my head and ran my fingers through my hair and dusted the grass off my clothes. The luxury of dreaming during the day is only available to the jobless. People with jobs do not get good sleep even at night due to the stress and tension that comes as an accompaniment with their job.

I forced myself to stand up and walk back to my make shift home at the railway station. The walk to the station was an ordeal that seemed to be never ending. I was dragging myself only with sheer determination as I just had the last remnants of energy left in my weak body. I stopped on the way to call my parents. Everything was like a dream as I was too tired and did not know where I was walking. I was so drowsy that it felt like I was walking in my sleep. I managed to reach a shopping area close to the railway station. I called my parents from a phone booth at the shopping complex.

"How are things with you Suraj? Are you able to get good food in the city? Did you manage to get a job, Suraj? Are you still sleeping on the platform?" Ma enquired.

I did not want to disappoint her or hide the facts from her so I said to her, "Ma, this is a long list of questions to be answered. Please do not worry about me. I am fine and really comfortable here. I am able to eat well. As for the job, I was either probably not the person they had in mind for the job or it was their misfortune that they lost a very sincere and hard working employee!!"

"Do not lose hope son, tomorrow will be a brighter day for my 'Suraj', she said in a soft loving voice with an even softer tone. "Life and fortune never remain stagnant Suraj, you will see how things change and they will surely change for the better my son. I am sure that there is something marvellous waiting for you ahead. Your dreams will come true very soon. I will pass it to your father now, he wants to talk to you," she said gently and we chatted a little before I said bye to her and Papa.

My mother's words were like a cool waterfall that washed away my tiredness with its gentle shower. Papa was in his usual 'Sermon Shower' mood so he guided me on how I could look for a job and the typical qualities employers look for in their prospective employees. I could not speak to them for long as it cost a lot for long distance calls so I had to cut short the call soon. I held on to the phone receiver for a long time even after I had disconnected the call and slid it into its cradle with great care and reluctance. My parents had made life very happy and comfortable for me but I had chosen to step out of the zone of my comfort and this pain of separation was the price I had to pay for it. I fondled the phone as it was the only link to my parents now. I was hoping to find a job soon and buy a mobile phone so that my dependency on phone booths could get reduced and I would call them any time and from anywhere with my phone. And this meant I had to be in a job and earn enough to buy a mobile phone. I was out of the shelter of my cool cocoon and it was not an easy life outside in the baking sun. I was again seeing myself running in the fields with a kite in my hand. The kite was flying high behind me and I was running with joy through the fields. I wanted to break free from all restrictions that were keeping my dreams away from me. I wanted to rise against the winds like my kite and let myself loose to fly into the vastness of the open blue sky.

Chapter 6

My father Shashi Pal is a very gentle and religious person who likes to visit the famous temples across the country. His favourite is the 'Shiv Shakti Puranik Mandir' of Murli. This has made him very spiritual and a walking library and encyclopedia of religious teachings. He has been living in Murli since his childhood as my grandparents belonged to Murli. His regular visits to the holy places and contacts with spiritual leaders and saints have made him a 'Sermon Shower' as I have named him. He gets into the 'Sermon Shower' mood and spends hours talking about spirituality, the powers of God, principles of a righteous life and famous legends of the Gods. It is good to hear his sermons occasionally but they get boring when they turn into a daily or hourly affair.

He had been working at the local post office as a supervisor for twelve years before he decided to move to farming to help his father. He had finished his schooling from Murli and had attended college at Devon before he returned to take up the job at the post office. He is very good at Mathematics and Accounts and I seem to have inherited this aptitude from him. He can walk for miles together and still have the stamina for a marathon. I am an ardent admirer of his stamina. He credits this to his good healthy diet that was regulated by my grandmother in his childhood. His diet is not as healthy now as he does not pay much attention to it neither does he heed to the doctor's advice. Yes, he had to recently visit the local doctor for his breathlessness and has been asked to lose some weight but he does not want to do much about it except binge on my mother's good cooking. He is very methodical in whatever he does without missing the minutest detail even if it means polishing his shoes or cleaning his bicycle. Watching my father polish his shoes is fun as it seems the shoes will wear out by the time my father is satisfied about their spotless sheen. He keeps brushing them with long and short strokes in all directions till the shoe is shining well enough to reflect his image. The brush and the shoe must both be tired and panting at the end of the ordeal. They must be thanking their stars when my father decides to wear his flip flops. And to watch him clean the bicycle is like watching an artist rehearse for a play as he makes sure that each and every part of the cycle is cleaned, at least five times before he declares it, 'Clean', like the artist rehearsing several times for a scene till the director shouts, 'Cut'. He has the patience to rub the handles, the bars, the spokes, the wheels, and the light for an hour or even more till he is convinced that they are as clean as new. And all this effort to drive it through the muddy roads of the fields again and get it dirty within ten minutes!

We were living as a joint family together with my grandparents 'Dada' and 'Dadi'. My father, like me, is also the only child of his father. My grandfather passed away when I was twelve years old and then my grandmother died when I was fifteen. Our home seemed so empty after my grandparents had gone. It took us a long time to accept the fact that they were not going to return and to accept the vacuum their absence had created in our hearts and in our lives as well as in our home. These empty spaces remain hollow and remind you of the loss whenever there is a celebration or a reason to feel happy or there is some joyous news to be shared. I would particularly remember them on my birthdays. I can point to every corner of the house and recount incidents from their lives that took place at those spots.

My Dada and Dadi loved me a lot and that showed in all their actions whether they got some snacks or sweets or clothes for me or played with me or read stories and fables to me. My Dadi loved to rock me when I was a child. She would sing lullabies to me and make me sleep in her arms. I can feel her soft cheeks against mine whenever I think about my childhood. The warmth and glow in her cheeks became even more prominent when she smiled lovingly at me. My Dada liked to take me for a ride in the tractor and we would relish roasted corn while we drove to the fields. He would take me to the fields and we hogged on the sugarcane till we could not have any more. He would tell me stories from his childhood and narrate interesting incidents from his life to me as I listened to him with undivided attention. The anecdotes were so humorous that I would get cramps in my stomach from laughing continuously. Those days are as fresh in my memory as the rising sun in the morning. He had taught me the *Gayatri Mantra* as he believed that this *Mantra* had a lot of power in it. We would recite the mantra in the morning before we had our breakfast and then in the evening at dusk. Dadi was very jovial and very active unlike other women of her age. Dada too was also very active and very fond of sweets. We used to hide sweets from him when we learnt he had turned diabetic. He did not want to give up on sweets but Dadi made sure that he could not find them at home. Dada would find reasons to make frequent trips to the local market to go to the sweet shop. This angered Dadi leading to arguments between Dada and Dadi. It was interesting to watch them argue over a piece of sweet *mithai*.

My mother Karuna Pal is more practical in life. The hardships of her childhood have made her very strong and realistic. She does go to the temple but not as regularly as my father. She is simple and knows what she wants from life and how much she can get from it. She had finished school but did not go to college due to her parents' financial constraints. She is a lady of a strong will and determination and very practical in her approach to life. She is very optimistic and ready to face any challenge that life may throw open to her. I have named her 'Stainless Steel' as she is the most strong and courageous person I have ever met in my life. She likes to knit and sew. She knits for all of us through the summers so that we can have new cardigans every winter. She recycles the old cardigans into new ones so we get to wear new woollens made from old wool. She is a very fine cook and that is the secret to my father's ever growing paunch. We overeat every single day as she puts all her love in her cooking. I have always seen her overly occupied with household chores and she never gets tired of running around the house. She does much more than what her age allows her to do. I admire her will and determination. She has been gifted with a melodious voice which we get to hear when she sings the *bhajans* for her prayers in the morning. Her voice has a soothing effect on my mind and soul. She is an artist in the making as she paints the pitchers and flower pots with water colours extremely well. She paints flowers and figurines on the pitchers and uses them to decorate the patio. The painted flower pots adorn the entrance to our home where they are lined up on the sides of the gate.

Her parents live in a nearby town called Jhilmil. Jhilmil is a town famous for its breathtaking lake and super delicious *samosas*. She moved to Murli when she married my father. I call her 'Ma' and I call my father 'Papa'. I am a lot like her in my appearance and that makes me fairer than my father. And I have inherited my built from my father that gives me a tall and stout disposition making me look a little older than my age. I feel fortunate for having inherited the best from both my parents.

We always looked forward to visiting my maternal grandparents 'Nana' and 'Nani' at Jhilmil. Boating at the lake was a daily activity followed by the mouth watering *samosas* from Guptajee's shop in the main bazaar in the heart of the town. There were times when we even had hot syrupy *jalebis* with the hot *samosas* and chutney. There were times when we added *chole* to the *samosa* and chutney menu. My grandparents doted on me and I was allowed to play all day long with the children from the neighbourhood. They did not nag me for not finishing my home work and that made them my favourite too. I waited for summer vacations every year to visit them at Jhilmil. Even though my parents believed that my grandparents were spoiling me by giving in to my tantrums, the trips to Jhilmil were a real vacation for me as I had the freedom to be myself throughout my stay at Jhilmil. My grandmother Nani's love would take the shape of *saag* and *makki ki roti* meal that she cooked for me. She would even make *matar samosas* for me. My grandfather Nana would take me boating and trekking near the lake.

He would tell me my favourite mythological stories from the epics. I would ask him to repeat the same stories over and over again and he never got tired of obliging me and that was his way of loving me immensely. I would sit on his lap and listen to all the stories he narrated to me in his soft deep voice. He modulated his voice with the flow of the stories and made them interesting each time I listened to them. I could hear them over and over again without getting bored or tired. He seemed to live through the stories as he narrated them to me. Nana and Nani have aged with time and are confined to their home as my Nana does not keep well and is too old to work.

Our home at Murli is literally humble. It is a simple and ordinary two room house with a kitchen and living room and two bathrooms. There is a decent patio in the front and a small backyard. The interiors are very modestly done up with bare minimum necessities of life. The furniture is old and simple. Some of the furniture is even older than my father in age. My bed is as old as my Dada. It was bought by my great grandfather when my Dada was born. I inherited it on my birth and we are still using it. The wood is as good as new. The fans in the house were also bought by my great grandfather and are still up and running; old is definitely gold. Their speed has slowed down gradually over the years but they are still running. Our home was built by my great great grandfather himself. He was an artisan and had built our home with his own hands brick by brick. It is named after him and is called Inderlok after his name Inder Pal. Each and every thing in the house has a story that dates far back into history. We did not believe in renovation or refurbishing and neither did our financial status allow us to do so. We had been content with whatever we had inherited from our forefathers. We had a visiting cat, I call it visiting as we had not kept it as a pet but it liked to visit us off and on. Cats, I learn, are attached to the house and not to the owners so this cat must have liked our house to visit it so often. There was a small bowl kept in the patio for her which was generously topped with milk on her visit to our home. This bowl also dates back to my great great grandfather's life time. The cat though was very new to this world. So we had an antique bowl at the disposal of a new cat for relishing regular meals of milk. This cat disappeared some days before I moved out of Murli. We were not sure whether it was still alive or if it had found another home that it preferred to ours. Our home sufficed for the three of us and was fully packed when my grandparents were alive. We had to accommodate our beds on the floor if we had guests visiting us. Our house is small but our hearts are very large to welcome whoever comes to visit us, whether a friend or relative or a stranger. We do not compromise on our hospitality for anyone. The cows were in a barn adjacent to our home. The cows were the responsibility of both Ma and Papa. I did not contribute much in that area of our life. I am not as methodical as Ma and Papa so they preferred that I did not attend to the cows. It was a herculean task to maintain the livestock. Ma took care of their food and Papa managed the barn. Life for Ma and Papa was tough and busy in spite of Murli being a lazy dazy town. Ma and Papa were surely an odd exception to the lazy crowd at Murli. Ma and Papa have led a simple life and I wanted to add comfort and luxury to it. I had moved out of Murli but the thoughts of my home were very fresh in my mind and I felt I was living through them once again as I turned the pages of my life.

$\mathcal{C}$hapter 7

I returned to my make shift home on the platform bench at night only to find another claimant to my bench spread out like a king size blanket on it. I looked hopefully at him with a gaze that would encourage him to move aside and make place for me but he ignored me blatantly and turned his face away. I wanted to roll him like a blanket and put him on a corner of the bench but such wishes seldom get fulfilled. I could not ask him to vacate my make shift home as he was as homeless as I was and the bench was unfortunately a public property. I kept staring at him waiting for a desirable response but all in vain. He was totally unmoved and showed no willingness to move. He pretended not to see me standing there.

I was annoyed by his presence but I still smiled imagining the person folded as a blanket. He was rolled well enough to have his nose stuck in his stomach and his feet were way up in the air and he was curled up to look like a spring roll that wore shoes. I imagined him as a sleeping bag with shoes and I smiled again and sat down next to the bench with my grey bag serving as my pillow and sleep took over in no time and I woke up the next morning to the hissing and huffing noise from a train leaving the station only to find the bench next to me vacant. "The guy could have at least nudged me to take over the bench when he was leaving", I thought, but people are not always as considerate as you would expect them to be. He had denied me the sleep on my new found bench house and left without even a sign of gratitude. "How thankless," I mumbled to myself and looked up at the brilliant blue skies. The skies had an aquamarine tinge welcoming me to a fresh and brand new day. "It is going to be a good day indeed," I convinced myself.

"God, be with me," I prayed before I commenced my morning ablutions. I changed into my spare set of clothes that were just a little better than the ones I was wearing at night. It was Day Fifteen in Gaulpur. I had washed at the platform restroom and moved with my singular agenda of finding a job that would help me buy my food and a rented accommodation. I recited the *Gayatri Mantra* before stepping out of the platform. *"Om bhurbhuvah swaha tatsavitur vareniyam bhargodevasya dheemahee dhiyo yo naah pracho dayat."* I recited the *mantra* eleven times before setting cruise for the day.

I did not have much experience on hand that could make me look like the best candidate for any job but I did have a willingness to make the best of any job offered to me. I was not giving up easily and of course life did not give me any other option to choose from. I was ready to take on multiple part time jobs at a time but there seemed to be a sudden dearth of jobs that could accommodate me. I was willing to work overtime and put in sixteen to eighteen hours of work in a day but there was nobody requiring my services. I was wandering in the streets of Gaulpur like a lost animal. The sense of dismay makes me go astray at times but I soon find ways to bounce back to optimism and determination to take charge of myself. I was soon in charge and let my feelings take a back seat as

I told myself that things are definitely going to get better and I had very little time to feel sorry for myself. I was empowering myself with all the optimism that I could garner from within myself. I pumped up my confidence, picked up my grey bag and retrieved and refreshed my smile and set out for the day. I walked towards a different direction from the platform and headed towards a new locality in search of a job.

*C*hapter 8

I found a new street to search for my dream job this time. This street was lined with numerous stores and offices. I had to cast my net wider to get a job as my efforts till now had been futile so I designed a new strategy for the day and that was to start from one end of the street and check for vacancies with each and every store and office till I reach the end of the street. I was not going to skip any store or office till I found a job for myself. I called out to God for help and sought His blessings before I set out for the day's journey and knock on every possible door that I could see. I had set out on my life's mission and told myself that I was going to return victorious. Positive begets positive so I was trying to generate positive energy by saying positive things so that I could hear some positive news. I was reciting the *Gayatri Mantra* as I walked towards the first store on the unusually busy street.

I first strolled into 'Balaji General Store', a grocery store. The store had a big board that was tilted towards the left and I could have almost hit my head with it as it was hung very low. The store was well lit and over stocked with groceries. The shelves were overly stuffed with groceries that made them look like an extra large size person bulging out from a medium size trouser. I browsed the whole shop as I walked towards the cash counter.

There were goods lying precariously on top shelves like someone standing on the tip of the diving board waiting to jump into the deep end of the swimming pool. The counters had not been dusted for a long time as they flaunted thumb marks on the lining of dust that covered them. I was looking around when I heard someone walk up too close to me. I saw a pair of droopy eyes staring at me with a thousand questions jumbled up in them eager to pop out one by one like a downpour of question marks flowing down from them in a stream. The owner of the shop stood there looking at me with his droopy eyes and grey hair questioning me as to what was it that I wanted to buy from his store. I was the first person to enter his store and that had made me special for the day as it is believed that good earnings from the first customer determine the sales trend for the day. The man had drooping shoulders together with his droopy eyes that must have come from his old age. He moved from the counter to a grocery shelf at the speed of a snail and pulled at one of the packets there. It seemed that all the packets on the shelf would immediately land on the floor and crack like raw eggs but they did not. The old man was very cautious as he pulled the packet out without disturbing the other packets that were squeezed into the shelf with it. He was dressed in a black and white check shirt, brown pants and black shoes like a penguin and he did walk like one too. The buttons on his shirt were broken and not done up properly; his shoes had not been polished since the day they were bought and his trousers had never been ironed. I again drifted into my dreams and imagined myself as the store supervisor getting the store cleaned and arranging the shelves neatly. I was counting the currency notes at the cash counter when my dream was interrupted by the man who asked if I needed help in finding what I was looking for. I was startled as I was woken up from my dream and it took me some time to come to terms with reality.

"Sir, I am not a customer I am here in search of a job. Do you need any helper for your store or an assistant who can help you with your book keeping?"

The man shrugged his shoulders and waved his head from left to right and replied, "No, nothing here, I am over staffed already and do not need anyone."

I could not believe him as the condition of the store spoke for itself. I could see that the old man was managing the store all by himself. He looked disheartened to know that I was not a customer. I could see the marks of disappointment painted vividly on his aging face. He must have run this shop for decades and waited each day for the first customer to appear and start the cash register flowing. I had brought him visible grief by entering his store at the wrong time of the day. I felt sorry for him and moved out slowly from the store leaving him grappling with his growing disappointment.

The next store was a meat shop called 'Mutton Chops'. I knocked at the door and opened it slowly for fear of coming face to face with a dead animal. I took five steps and was inside the shop with red meat hanging all around me. The table in front was covered with meat packets and some meat cans and a few knives. The shop was unkempt and the smell of dead carcasses was unbearable. I had to hold my breath to walk to the person in charge of the shop. I approached the person and asked him if I could get a job in his shop. The man was holding a mammoth knife that looked like a sword in his hand and he pointed it towards me and said in a deep grunting tone, "I do not keep anyone to help me," and returned to his chopping board. The man was tall and stout with extra long hands that held the sword like knife just like one would hold a broom. I looked around the shop and saw dead meat all around me. It was a ghastly site for me as I am a vegetarian. It was not easy asking for work at this shop but I still did because I was not sure whether this was the opportunity that God would want me to pick so that He could chart the course of my life from here. So I tried to make the man understand how I could be of use at the shop but he had made up his mind. He was sure that he did not need any help around the store and his body language conveyed his decision with absolute conviction. The man kept chopping meat at amazing speed like a squirrel thrashing a nut with his head bouncing up and down with an equal velocity. His face was as expressionless and as dead as the meat in his shop. I left the shop and moved to the next store. I am a firm believer in God so whenever I am faced with such a situation I tell myself that God did not help me here because He has something better in store for me. I repeated this in my head two to three times and it was a great consolation for me and I set out to find the golden opportunity which God had designed for me to trace the future path of my life. I recited the *Gayatri Mantra* in my mind before making a grand entry into the next store.

The third store was a ladies's garment outlet 'Kamini'. I entered the store to the sound of heavy metallic music that was playing inside at the highest possible volume. I looked around the store but did not see anyone. I wandered in the store like a child set free in toy land. These colourful garments were made by reputed designers whose labels were sewn on to the fabric. I tried looking at the price tags of the women's dresses and was shocked to see a garment priced at fifty five thousand rupees. My hand pulled away from the dress as if it had touched a live electric wire. I looked at my two hundred rupee shirt and felt its fabric. I tried to compare the fabric of the dress with my shirt and could not comprehend the reason for the dress to be so overpriced. I suddenly felt very poor! I was not just poor but the poorest soul under the sky! I would need to sell my land back home to buy such a dress. The women in this city must be crazily rich to afford such clothes. Or they were married to the richest landlords who could afford to buy them such expensive dresses. I noticed a trial room at the back of the store and today I can laugh at what I had done that day. I picked up the dress and went into the trial room to try it on. I wanted to feel rich so I wore it. It was a funny feeling wearing a ladies' dress. The dress was too tight and did not even reach my knees and it cost so much that it was shocking for me to believe that clothes can be so expensive. The cost of this little piece of fabric was sufficient to buy me clothes for a lifetime. I fitted myself in the dress and walked around the store baring my hairy bear like legs. I felt silly wearing a ladies' dress. I tried to take it off after a few minutes but to my horror the dress would not budge. It was too tight for me to even breathe as it was not meant for a masculine figure. I had a tough time trying to roll it one centimeter at a time and pull it over my head. Half way through I was unable to move the dress even a millimeter. I wriggled and twisted and wriggled and twisted myself multiple times and pulled at the dress and it seemed like ages before I could make it move up. It was an ordeal to come out of the dress and I was perspiring by the time I had it off. I heard some stitches coming off as I pulled my arms out of its sleeves. I wondered how women fit into such tight clothes. I kept the dress back from where I had picked it up and waited for the store owner to come but no one appeared from the front or the back gate of the store so I decided to try my luck at the fourth store which was an ice cream parlour. Just when I was walking out of the garment store I heard frantic footsteps behind me and I turned around to see an old lady dressed in white moving quickly towards me. "You there", she shouted. My heart missed a beat and then it started to accelerate on hearing her voice. I could hear my heart beat like a railway engine running at full speed. "Are you the courier boy?" she asked. I sighed and calmed myself on hearing her question. I thanked my stars for having saved me. I was startled on hearing her voice as I thought she might have seen me with the dress but was soon at ease when I heard her asking for the courier boy. "No Ma'am, I am not the courier boy", I replied. "Oh, I thought you were, never mind. But what are you doing here?" she enquired with her right eyebrow moving high up to touch her forehead. "I am looking for a job and wanted to know if there is any vacancy in this store." "Not currently, we are not hiring anyone," she answered with a suspicious look on her face. I nodded and left the store.

I slipped out of 'Kamini' and moved to the 'Kool Kones' ice cream parlour next door. I was tempted by the aroma and colour of different ice cream flavours at the parlour. The ice cream tubs displayed at the counter left me craving for an ice cream. I went into my dream world once again and was handing out ice cream cones to school children and other customers. I wore the chef's cap that had a red edge and an apron that had a red and white check print on it. I was standing behind the counter and constantly scooping out ice cream from the ice cream tubs.

Suddenly the counter was filled with melted ice cream and I picked up a towel to clean the counter. I woke up from my dream on feeling the glass lining of the counter as I lifted my hand to pick up the towel. I pulled my hand back and moved towards the lady at the cash counter of the parlour. I tried to avoid looking at the counter when I spoke to the lady at the cash desk. The ice cream was tempting but I did not give in to the temptation. The lady was counting the currency notes and seemed to ignore me. She kept nodding her head and I was unsure as to whether the nod was due to her counting the cash or was it an acknowledgement of what I had told her. I looked around to see two tables and eight chairs laid out in the middle of the shop for customers to sit and relish the ice cream. The red menu on display was new and shiny. I read the menu from start to finish three times while the lady kept nodding and counted the notes. I waited for her to finish counting the cash and asked her for any job requirement at the parlour. She looked up and swayed her head to the other corner of the store. I looked towards the corner and saw someone sitting on a stool. I assumed him to be the store owner and walked up to him and repeated my question. The man was chewing tobacco and looked disinterested in talking to me. I was waiting for an answer but his answer was stuck between the chewed tobacco and his teeth. He tried gripping the tobacco in his mouth with his chin high up in the air to stop the tobacco drool from dripping on him and shook his head in a refusal mode. His words were lost somewhere in the chewed tobacco that he had stuffed his mouth with. I wondered why people chew tobacco when it can cause deadly diseases like cancer and chokes their words making them mute most of the time. My dream of dressing up as an ice cream man with an apron and chef's cap was shattered within a moment by him. I looked at the ice cream tubs again and bid farewell to them with a heavy heart. I had some money in my pocket but I resisted buying a scoop as I had to save the money for the very essentials and contingencies. I was disappointed for a few minutes but soon gathered my wits and walked out gracefully like a defeated sportsman.

One store after another, I had visited four stores and the next was an office. This office was on the third floor of a building next to Kool Kones. The building was new and did not house any other establishment except this office apart from one more office that was under renovation. This office was a sports goods trading company called 'Sports Whiz'. I climbed up three floors and reached the office. I entered through the wooden door of the office and repeated my regular statement, "Sir, I am looking for a job and want to know in case there is any requirement in your office. I can work as your assistant and help with your book keeping. I can take up any job Sir." I was asked to wait at the reception.

It was two in the afternoon and I did not hear from anyone till four p.m. I spent these two hours looking at the magazines placed in a rack at the reception of the office. There were two ladies at the reception, one was busy with her computer and the other one was on the phone. An office boy kept making an appearance from within the office with either a bunch of files or with some water or tea for the ladies. I looked around the reception and noticed a display unit with photographs of sports goods and sports equipments. I walked up to it and read the entire details ten to twelve times. Then I read the notice backwards a couple of times till I had memorized it fully. There was an exclusive desk that was stationed near the reception for sale of sample goods. It was a two hours long wait at the reception till a lady called for me. The lady asked me why I was there and I continued harping about all that I could do and that I was willing to take up any type of job. It was again a big 'No' from this office. I was dreaming of standing behind the sales counter selling sports gear to famous sportsmen and taking their autographs when I heard the door close behind me and I was standing at the landing of the winding staircase.

I was clueless as to why they had made me wait for so long if they did not want to hire me. The only positive aspect that I could find in the long wait was that I was away from the hot sun in the comfort of a cool air conditioned room for two hours. I was getting dejected so I chanted the *Gayatri Mantra* to calm myself down and started to descend from the staircase.

I was lost in my thoughts and climbed down slowly with my mind running through the sequence of events of the entire day. The staircase was as winding as my thoughts that rushed from one thing to another and back as I descended to the ground floor.

Chapter 9

I was climbing down the last flight of the staircase when I spotted an old man standing near the main entrance door of the building. As I approached the main door I realized that the old man was old but not as old as he had looked from a distance. The wrinkles on his face were very well pronounced. I was impressed by his demeanor as he stood there straight and elegant in an expensive suit and shoes and with an even more expensive smart phone in his well manicured hand. His grey hair enhanced his grace. His shoes had an impeccable shine that conveyed that they had just been polished. He wore a gold ring that flashed each time he moved his hand and made a shining halo on the wall in front. He had an extremely positive aura that attracted me. He was a man of substance! He was the man whom I would want as my ideal. He looked like a very successful person who had the world dancing to his tunes. The platinum frame of his spectacles defined his eyes and made them look very deep and focused. His wrist watch seemed to be more expensive than his gold ring and expensive suit. His persona was oozing abundance of exuberance luxuriously. He had the height of a King and so were his built and his presence. My admiration for the old man was soon interrupted by another man who came running down the stairs shouting

"Mehta Sir", "Mehta Sir!" The old man aka Mehta Sir did not seem to acknowledge the man's presence and his calm face was slowly turning red with streaks of anger lighting up his cheeks. The folds on his forehead were increasing with the intensity of his anger. His eyes were turning red like fire in a fuming furnace. The graph of his anger was definitely growing exponentially with steam rising in all possible directions from the axes of the graph. He was in the worst mood that one can be in.

He turned around to look at the man and said, "Prem, where is the driver?" Prem was silent. I could tell Mehta Sir was going to lose it. Prem was determined to get a scolding from Mehta Sir and kept silent for a long time. It must have been some seconds but the silence made it seem never ending. Prem fidgeted and shifted from one foot to the other and his arm seemed to tweak a bit after every ten seconds. He had a glum look on his face which was permanently glued to it like an old movie poster on a wall. His reactions were not in tune with the situation at hand. He stood there in silence waiting like some bait for the beast to devour. His arm was shifting with a frequent jerk like the seconds arm of a clock. He could not stand still even for a moment and that made him look like a person trying to balance himself on roller skates for the first time. He surely appeared to be an awkward personality who did not have many bones to support his tall skeleton. He was tilting towards one side as he finally tried to respond to Mehta Sir but his reply decided to stay put in the server of his throat and he stretched his neck to look outside the gate towards the car parked in front of the building. He seemed to have stretched his neck too far as the distance between the tip of his nose and his shoulder had suddenly increased leaving him look like the letter 'L' that had been totally inverted. Prem was tense, confused and scared and of course as silent as silence can be.

Mehta Sir squeezed his eyes and looked at Prem again, "Driver!!! Where is he, Prem???"

Prem trembled and let out a whisper, "He has quit Sir."

Mehta Sir's eyebrows lifted upwards as he growled, "Who is taking me home then?"

He happened to notice me as he growled and his gaze focused on me for a few seconds. I realized I was still standing near the door and had forgotten my mission of marching on the streets in my usual job hunt parade. The conversation had become so engrossing that I almost became a part of it and wanted to hear it till the end. I was glued to my spot and did not want to walk out of the building. I stood there like the audience in a movie hall waiting to see some action. I wanted to see Mehta Sir punch Prem but my wish remained unfulfilled.

"No respect for time, you guys have no respect for time," exclaimed Mehta Sir. "Utterly disgusting staff that I have here," Mehta Sir continued. "Do I pay you for keeping silent Prem?" Mehta Sir questioned Prem.

Prem kept silent. He was surely a very annoying man. I was surprised how a person like Mehta Sir could put up with this man who was nothing but utter nuisance. Prem must be good at his work otherwise there is no reason why such a graceful man like Mehta Sir would tolerate his presence.

"Job", I mumbled and Prem's words echoed in my ears "He has quit Sir." "Quit, did he say quit? Had Mehta Sir's driver quit?" "Did I hear it right?" I asked myself. "Did he really say Quit?" I asked myself again and believed that I had heard him correctly. "Think fast Suraj, think fast,"

I said to myself. My brain was working overtime and I was seeing a vacancy, a job, a house and my dream of making it big. I pressed the pause button of the video of my daydreaming reluctantly and tried to catch Mehta Sir's attention.

"Sir, I can drive you back home if you permit me Sir." I blurted out with the speed of an express train and held my breath as I waited for a response but I was greeted with silence. The silence seemed endless as there was a long pause so I repeated myself, "Sir, I can drive you back home if you permit me Sir."

Mehta Sir looked at me and asked, "Do you have a driving license?" I was speechless. I did not understand whether it was a Yes or a No. I was trying to comprehend Mehta Sir's statement when he repeated himself, "Driving license??" I reached for my grey bag and dug in it's pocket to dish out my driving license. This was the first time in my life that I was pleased with the fact that I owned a driving license. This piece of article lay in my bag with no importance till that day but suddenly it seemed like a gateway to my dreams. I thanked the day when my friend Raja had suggested me to get a driving license made for myself.

Mehta Sir glanced at the license and nodded, "Ok, drive me home, Suraj Pal, but No Mistakes, I repeat, No Mistakes!!" I shook my head in a gratifying nod, Mehta Sir turned to Prem, Mehta Sir's ring flashed again, it's shining halo danced on the wall, Prem apprehensively felt for the car keys in his pocket, pulled them out and handed them over to me. I held the car keys with great pride as if I was holding my dream in my hand. I felt the metallic touch of the car keys and seemed like the owner of the black luxury sedan in which I was taking Mehta Sir

'Home'. I was caressing the keys when I noticed Mehta Sir looking askance at me as I had not moved from my place. I quickly gathered myself and walked towards the car. It was a beauty, shining black metal with silver wheels waiting to take off like a jet. I had driven smaller cars and utility vehicles from farms to grain markets back home in my small town. Those trips were majorly for adventure and less for the little money I used to get from the farmers but here in Gaulpur, it could be for a living. I held the car door with great pride as Mehta Sir slid into his seat. Prem followed him and got into the seat next to Mehta Sir. I got into the driver's seat of the plush car with my heart thumping with nervousness. I was in the driver's seat and held the steering wheel with great pride and passion as one would hold a fortune. I had to be careful while driving as this was a priceless car. I turned the ignition key with my trembling hands and moved the car around slowly. The sound from the engine was like a prayer being answered by God Himself. Prem directed me to Mehta Sir's 'Home' as I drove his luxury car. I had forgotten Murli and Gaulpur and my dreams; I was on cloud nine and in seventh heaven as this was a journey of super style and extravaganza. I was floating in the sky amidst the white clouds and the car was moving on its own. I did not want to stop at any traffic signal as that would spoil my dream. We were lucky to get clear traffic and there were no red signals on our route. I learnt from Mehta Sir and Prem's conversation that they owned the office that was under renovation in the building where I had met them and they had come to meet the architect at their new office.

Twenty minutes later we entered a huge wooden gate that had lions and elephants carved on it. The gate was opened by two guards who bowed and saluted Mehta Sir. We drove through an arcade of lush green trees lined on both sides of the long driveway that culminated into a beautiful porch with a fountain in the centre. The fountain had exquisite mermaid statues around it and a flower bed at its base. I had never seen such a beautiful house in my life before. The water in the fountain stream was so clear that the mermaids' reflections made them look real. The sound of the stream of the fountain was very soothing and refreshing as I felt rejuvenated on hearing it. I jumped out of the car and opened the door for Mehta Sir who seemed a little tired from the ride. I looked around and was wonderstruck by the beauty of the Mansion. I seemed to have reached a heaven on Earth. Jalpari was nothing compared to this Mansion. This Mansion was beauty and royalty of the highest order. I was amazed by the beautiful surroundings. The magnificence of the Mansion had me awe struck. My neck kept moving from one end to the other trying to feast my eyes on the beauty of the Mansion. The Mansion was like a palace out of a fairy tale. I was admiring the Mansion when I heard someone come out of the main gate and that brought me back to reality. My journey of being 'The King' had soon come to an end. I was not sure as to what lay ahead in life for me. I thought of leaving and looked at Mehta Sir. I was not expecting a goodbye from him but I just looked at him to say that I would be leaving now. "*Namaste* Sir, I will be leaving now," I told Mehta Sir as I turned towards the driveway. Mehta Sir's phone rang so he waved his hand asking me to wait for him to finish the call. I stood there admiring the beauty of the Mansion and its garden that had an absolutely stunning landscape. I was engrossed by the beauty around me and forgot that I was waiting for Mehta Sir. His call got over in a few minutes and he looked at me with a stream of varied emotions painted on his face as his mind seemed to race with multiple thoughts flowing through it.

$\mathcal{C}$hapter 10

Mehta Sir stood at the porch and looked at me. "Suraj, I liked the way you drove me at slow speed and I can see you are in need of a job and of course I know you are an honest man. I want you to work for me. You will drive me to my office daily."

I was taken aback. It came as a shock to me. I should have jumped up with joy at this news but it had come as a surprise so my reaction was not in consonance with the news. I was expecting to say goodbye to Mehta Sir but this reaction from him was unexpected and I was too excited to utter anything. I managed to collect my wits and thanked him. "Thank you Sir, thank you so much for considering me worthy of this job. I will not disappoint you Sir. Thank you so much Sir," I said to Mehta Sir in my excitement. Mehta Sir just let his head move slightly in a nod.

His words were like a prayer being answered by God. My heart fluttered at the very thought of having bagged my first job in Gaulpur. My biggest tension was calmed by Mehta Sir's statement. I was surprised at how he could pass a judgement about me within thirty minutes of our meeting. "Age and experience do make a person wise," I told myself as I let the feeling of happiness and relief settle within me.

Prem was standing in silence again and glanced at me with his glum face. He was as dead as the floor beneath him and as silent as the pillar he was standing next to. He could have merged with the background and nobody would have noticed him. He was indeed a 'Vegetable' that tagged along with Mehta Sir. I was curious to find out why Mehta Sir tolerated his presence.

"Mani", Mehta Sir called out and I saw a man coming from the East end of the garden. Mani was a man of small built and dark complexion and a semi bald head and as I got to know him I also found him to have a good sense of humour in addition to a kind hearted nature. Mani rolled into the porch with his big kangaroo paunch that dived in before he could. He was panting from the race from the garden to the porch.

"Mani," said Mehta Sir, "Suraj is my new driver, show him his quarters. Let him know about his wages."

I thanked Mehta Sir. My heart thanked Mehta Sir's old driver who had quit his job to create a vacancy for me. He was God's helping hand for me that day!! I could have thanked him a million times. I asked God to grant him all his wishes.

"Quarters, did I hear Mehta Sir correctly? Did he say quarters? That would be another prayer answered by God. I wish what I had just heard is true and I am going to get a place to stay together with this job," I spoke to myself. I could feel that God had especially come to help me and was standing there with me and organizing my life as per my will. I thanked God again for relieving me of all my stress and tensions.

Mani waited to catch his breath, adjusted his shirt on his paunch, looked at me for some time and then asked me to follow him. Mani and I walked through the garden to the 'quarters'. The garden had a beautiful landscaping that gave it the feel of a valley. There were beautiful water fountains in the garden that had ornamental birds and squirrels on their brims. One of the trees had a number of bird houses hung on its branches. Some of the bird houses had nests in them from where I could hear the little fledglings chirping. The garden was full of life and I could feel myself merging in this life as I walked towards the dormitory. I knew I would soon wrap this life around me.

Mani looked at me and said, "Don't know how long will you last here! Drivers keep disappearing all the time." I chuckled, "I am here to stay for long, Mani, here to stay for long." "You will not get more than ten thousand rupees a month. Quarters and meals are a perk here. You will be at the beck and call of Mehta Sir. Hope you understand." I listened to him with my mouth open. "Ten thousand Rupees. He had said ten thousand rupees a month". I could not believe my ears. My excitement was pouring out of me in my smile. "Ten thousand Rupees?" I blurted out in astonishment. It sounded like a huge amount for a beginner. The day seemed to be very lucky indeed! Mani gave me a rough look and said, "Yes, ten thousand rupees and no more. That is the ongoing rate here and we will not give you more than that. Take it or leave it. The rate outside is much less but Mehta Sir is generous with his staff so he pays two to three thousand extra. Don't expect even a rupee more than that. Do you understand?" I nodded in agreement and smiled at him again. He again gave me a queer look that said he found me too weird. I was too happy to have this job that paid well and I also had a place to stay with free meals. I hopped behind Mani as he tumbled towards the servant quarters.

We walked past a gardener who was busy watering the plants. Mani called out to him, "Lakhan, how come you are out here in the evening. I thought you were not going to show up today." Lakhan looked up at Mani and smiled as he replied, "Mani, I will not be coming tomorrow so I thought of watering the plants in the evening as well." Mani laughed out loudly, "Water them again and again? Do you want to kill them with overdose of water?" Lakhan retorted, "I know what I am doing. I will not overdose them with water. I know how much they can take. They will survive, you need not worry. Each one of us has a capacity and I never exceed that capacity be it plants or men."

Mani smirked at him and we moved to the servant quarters. The servant quarters were located towards the West end of the Mansion and the porch of the Mansion could be seen from one side of the servant quarters. I counted eighteen beds in the huge dormitory and assumed at least eighteen servants must reside here. The room was well lit and the compound was enveloped by flowering trees and plants. I recited the *Gayatri Mantra* before I stepped into the dormitory. I was lucky to get a bed close to the window. I emptied the contents of my grey bag onto the bed and put them in the locker that Mani allotted to me in the dorm. Mani showed me the bathroom and my bed and told me that food gets served at the servant quarters' kitchen and I need to be there in time so I washed and reached the kitchen immediately for a good wholesome meal. The kitchen had a huge hall attached to it and I saw seven servants having their meal at that time. I presumed other servants must be busy with their work. This meal was the best meal of my lifetime. It was the first good meal that I had after landing in

Gaulpur. I was starving and the sight of food made me jump up with joy. I over ate as I had seen food after two weeks. I could sense that Mehta Sir must be a very kind man to provide food to all his servants. He was indeed very generous as I learnt gradually as I got to know him. I had eaten to my heart's content so I felt very drowsy. I lay on my bed for some time and lazed out for a while.

I was called by Mehta Sir after an hour. I had to take him to Broadway Plaza for a meeting. Broadway Plaza is a commercial hub in downtown Gaulpur where Mehta Sir owned three offices. Prem came along for the meeting with his unbreakable silence and dismal glum look. I was still trying to figure out if Prem was just a 'file holder', he only seemed to hold Mehta Sir's files and did not do anything apart from that. He was almost like an office bag for Mehta Sir. He did not seem to be doing more than that. I learnt after some days that he was a distant relative of the Mehtas and that was the reason for them to be putting up with him. My focus moved from Prem to myself. I was driving Mehta Sir in his luxury sedan again. I was looking forward to the evening when I would walk to a phone booth and call my parents to let them know about my job. They would be excited and relieved to get this news. I could not wait to tell Ma the good news and hear the excitement in her voice. We drove towards Broadway Plaza and I waited in the car while Mehta Sir and Prem went for the meeting.

I was finally employed!!

I spoke to my parents at length later in the evening from a phone booth near Mehta Mansion. They happy and relieved to know that I had found employment in the city. Ma chuckled as she spoke to me and Papa gave me some instructions before he blessed me. Ma's voice had a feeling of relief in it as she spoke to me. She was happy and at peace that things were falling in line for me. Ma was happy that I had a place to stay now and was even getting home made food. She could not stop thanking God for His timely and gracious help. I spoke to them for twenty minutes and returned to the Mansion. I had a sense of achievement around me as I walked from the Mansion gate to the dorm. I was at peace with myself.

Chapter 11

I had a great night sleep at my new home. No hissing, no whistles, no shouting from passengers and coolies and stall owners, no Buntea meals, no noise of running footsteps, no crouching on a bench, no shaking of the earth by moving trains; this place was heavenly. I was sleeping on a real bed after a long time. It was the first night after arriving in Gaulpur that I got to sleep soundly. I dreamt of the fields in Murli in my sleep. And of course I was with Ma and Papa in my dream. I got up refreshed the next morning and felt like a new person with renewed energy and enthusiasm. I woke up and did not find Sundar around me and was confused for a few moments as it was very quiet. It took me sometime to realize that I was not at the platform anymore. I was at my new home. I walked to the kitchen to get some tea. This was the first morning of my new life. The tea was very refreshing. The cook handed me a crisp *mathri* and cookies with a cup of tea. I was impressed with the care given to all the domestic help at Mehta Mansion.

I had begun to like the place within hours of moving into the quarters. I had a place to live that came with good meals and a job, what more could I have wished for? I thanked God for helping me when I needed it the most.

But there was more help to come from The Almighty as life soon revealed to me.

I could see the colourful Pansies and the white and red Plumeria trees in the garden from the window near my bed in the dormitory. It was a beautiful and breathtaking view that made each day special for me. Anita was even more special. Anita took care of Mrs. Mehta and I could see her walk to the porch from where I lived. She walked from the Mansion Gate to the porch every morning at eight and I would wait to see her till she disappeared into the house. I wanted to speak to Anita but could not gather my wits to approach her and talk to her. I admired her from a distance. She was my five feet tall dream that made me look forward to getting up early every morning. I did not need an alarm to wake me up as the very thought of getting a glimpse of Anita made me wake up at four every morning. Her presence brought cheer into my dull and listless life.

I had not seen the Mehta Mansion and yearned to take a tour of it. All I knew was that this Mansion was overflowing with luxury and wealth. Mehta Sir had businesses spread across industries and nations and each business was extremely successful. He owned a mansion in every major city and had many villas across all the States of the country. He seemed to have a kingdom of his own. God had been luxuriously generous in providing wealth to him. And he in turn was generous to us.

I was driving Mehta Sir around the city and getting a good salary for my job as his driver. He would rarely speak to me and I knew that driving at slow speed was the trick to keep him calm. I had seen him get angry at other servants when things were not up to his taste and standards so I ensured that I do not come in his bad books. I needed the job and of course it came with good perks like a comfortable place to live and good meals. I was contemplating ways to save a part of my wages so that I could build a corpus for my future. Life was comfortable but I was not content with it. I knew I was heading in the right direction but I was still too far from my goal.

I would drive Mehta Sir to various offices during the day. It was seldom that he would visit a single office in a day. He had his business spread across and that made him travel a lot. I had to drive him to nearby towns also. He used to take the flight only when the journey was to places beyond three hundred kilometers else he preferred to be driven in his car. I had an easy life when Mehta Sir travelled to far off locations. It was like a paid holiday for me but I spent that time in helping the other servants as I do not like to spend my time idling.

Mehta Sir owned sixteen cars and each one of them was an extraordinary beauty. He had one vintage car that he took pride in driving himself. He made me polish the vintage car every Sunday and he himself drove Mrs. Mehta to their Club near the Golf Course. There were times when he asked me to accompany them to the Club. I sat on the rear seat while he drove to the Club and then I got to park the royal vintage car in the Club's parking lot and that made me feel like a King. All the cars of Mehta family were parked behind the mansion in an area marked as the 'Garage Wing'. I had to spend the early morning hours in this area polishing the cars. I would spend some time admiring the cars as each one was better than the other and a beauty to behold. I had fallen in love with all of them at the same time. I wanted to drive each one around but Mehta Sir preferred to be driven in the same sedan during the day. He would change the car when we drove out of station or went to a party. There was another driver who drove Mrs. Mehta. Two more drivers were there for the guests who visited Mehta Mansion. Guests frequented the Mansion as Mehtas had a huge network of business associates, a big family and an even bigger friends and social circle.

$\mathscr{C}$hapter 12

I would speak to my parents often to let them know about my well being. They were happy for me and I knew they yearned to meet me though they had never explicitly expressed their desire to me in words. My parents were as usual making a living from farming at Murli. Life was tough and means were little but they were content with whatever life had to offer them. I had become discontented and that was the prime reason for me to move from Murli to Gaulpur. I had out grown from tilling and harvesting and my heart desired to explore the outside world for opportunities to fulfill my dream of having a luxurious life like the landlords of Murli. I had left Murli with two thousand rupees with me, a treasure that I had saved during the last five years. I also had blessings from my parents who had great expectations from me, their only child. I wanted to live up to their expectations and do something that would make them proud of me. I did not want to let life pass by me as I wanted to be different and make a difference.

Mrs. Mehta was an admirable lady who had not forgotten her humility, politeness and soft spoken nature in spite of the grandeur and wealth that surrounded her. She would tour the garden in the morning and see me polish the car in the porch while I waited for Mehta Sir.

Her smile was warm and her eyes had a blessing in them whenever she looked at me. She responded to me each time I greeted her. She occasionally inquired about my well being. Anita would accompany her during her walk to the garden and that made Mrs. Mehta's appearance at the porch even more special for me. Mrs. Mehta was a lady of an average built and lean body. Her face glowed from her positivity and her grey hair lent her an air of elegance. She had the grace of a swan as she walked through the porch to the garden. She had the stance of a queen which augmented her grace and elegance. She always carried her shawl with her irrespective of the weather. Her age must make her feel cold in the garden even in summers.

I used to sit with Lakhan in my spare time and watch him plant saplings and water and trim the plants. Lakhan gave life to the garden at Mehta Mansion. Lakhan's son Babul did not have the same expertise but was good at his work at the garden. Lakhan cared for the plants like one would care for his children. He was extremely possessive about them and got depressed at even the sight of a single wilting leaf. I liked to watch him work with his garden tools. He dug up the earth with such passion that it seemed that he was about to unearth a hidden treasure. He had trimmed some plants into the shape of animals. I particularly liked the plant that was trimmed like a bear as it had a funny little tail. He had a passion for trimming plants into various shapes. There was a bushy shrub that he had trimmed into the shape of a spiral and another one as a boat. He had a vivid imagination that he could easily translate into these shapes like one would pen down poetry on a sheet of paper or draw on a canvas. His scissors moved with such flair that its blades seemed to do a waltz in the air. He was God's own man! Lakhan and Babul had given the garden a beautiful and admirable life that reflected in every tree, flower, shrub and bush.

Anita was very fond of flowers and being with Lakhan gave me an opportunity to see her whenever she walked to the flower beds in the garden. She seemed to know all their names and impressed me and Lakhan with her knowledge about plants. She would particularly look for the orange gladioli and mauve pansies and stand there for a long time in admiration of their colour. I admired Anita as she would engross herself in admiring the beauty of the flowers. Her fingers matched the beauty of the petals that she held as she plucked the flowers. The sunshine made her sparkling eyes look prettier than the stars. She walked like an angel with happiness in the folds of her dreamy mystifying eyes. She looked astonishingly pretty as she walked around the Mansion and the garden like a fairy. Everything about her was so magical that it left me fascinated. The aura of her mesmerizing and magnetic personality left me spellbound.

I helped Lakhan in mowing the grass in my spare time. I liked to walk barefoot on the grass as I mowed it. The feel of the soft cut grass blades reminded me of my fields back home in Murli. I would hold my Murli in my thoughts as I walked on the grass. The drops of dew on the grass slipped on the blades and wet my feet as I felt the grass under my feet. I was a man of the Earth and that had me rooted to the grass and to my fundamental principles too which helped me in every decision that I took in my life. I liked to sit on the cot under the cool shade of the tall mango tree behind the dormitory. There was a kitchen garden in the backyard where Lakhan planted vegetables and fruits. The mango tree was on one edge of the kitchen garden where I used to sit on my cot during the afternoons when Mehta Sir was travelling out of station. Lakhan would give me company at times and enlighten me about the large number of varieties of mango. I would doze off listening to him but he continued talking about mangoes and other species of fruits as I dreamt about Murli. He would explain to me with great enthusiasm how and when each vegetable needs to be planted. He assumed that I had a lot of interest in gardening due to my farming background so I was his prime audience whom he liked to present his knowledge and skills to.

Mehta Sir owned two dogs, Joy and Polly, who led a life of royalty as they rode in sedans and ate the best pet foods brought from the best supermarkets and were always very well groomed. Their lifestyle could have made anyone envious of them. The Boxers Joy and Polly were dark brown and their coats were always neatly combed with care and expertise to lend them a dusky shine. They were not allowed to get friendly with the servants. Their trainer Rocky came twice a week and we would watch him train them. Rocky had a lot of patience as he repeated his instructions to Joy and Polly over and over again till they got attuned to them and followed them instantaneously. It was a funny site as it was the trainer Rocky who seemed to bark more frequently than the Boxers. Lakhan and I waited for a reaction from Joy and Polly each time Rocky barked or signaled to them. Our gaze shifted from him to the Boxers and back again and this continued till Rocky was confident that the Boxers had understood him well. Our necks went from left to right like a pendulum watching the three of them, Rocky, Joy and Polly as though we were witnessing a Tennis match in action.

I smiled each time I saw Rocky as I felt he would be most appropriate to help get a reaction out of Prem who was always glum and his responses were too slow that I doubted his ability to comprehend situations. I was imagining Rocky tugging at Prem's leash as he trained him. Prem kept a straight blank face as Rocky's face fumed in anger. Prem was difficult to train but Rocky kept shouting at him till he got Prem to react. Prem actually reacted and that was amazing. I wanted to applaud and hug Rocky for this incredible achievement. I was walking towards Rocky to shake hands with him when I heard someone call out my name. I stopped and again heard someone call out my name and looked around to see Prem standing behind me. I had a smirk on my face as I looked at Prem. I tried to look for his leash and his dog ears but could not see them in their place. Prem called out my name again. I came out of my daydreaming and noticed that Prem's leash was not in its place and his tail had stopped wagging too. I turned around and saw Rocky playing ball with Joy and Polly. I turned back to Prem and smiled at him while he gave me a blank glance. I was in a state of mixed emotions like someone who has watched a comedy movie that had a tragic ending. "Such is life," I told myself. "It is rare to have happy endings in real life," I thought with great disappointment. I really wanted to see Prem fetch the ball and stand on his hind legs. I was disappointed with Prem for having distracted me from my comic dream.

Prem asked me to bring the car to the porch as Mehta Sir had to leave for a meeting. I walked to the garage in amusement. My day dreaming was a habit that had grown with me over the years. It did not take me any time to drift into my dreams. It took a few minutes for me to start hallucinating and fantasizing like a small child playing a pretend game. It was an entertaining pastime for me. I got into the car and turned the ignition to pull the car out of the garage and into the porch. The sound of the rolling engine was always music to my ears as it lifted my spirits and transported me into another world. I parked the car in the porch and got out to open the door for Mehta Sir who was waiting for the car. Mehta Sir got in and Prem followed him. I again smiled at Prem. I could not get over my dream and found Prem to be very amusing. I could have held his leash and taken him for a walk. We drove out of town to the outskirts of Gaulpur to a BPO where Mehta Sir had a meeting. I was waiting at the parking lot when I saw a familiar face. The man coming out of the building looked a lot like Raja. Yes, it was Raja indeed! I jumped up with excitement to see Raja. I could not believe my eyes that I was seeing him in Gaulpur.

Chapter 13

"Raja, Raja, look here, it is me, Suraj," I shouted loudly to gain his attention and waved my hands in the air like an orchestra Director. Raja turned around and looked astonishingly at me. He bolted towards me. I ran and met him halfway. We hugged each other. I picked him up and circled myself while hugging him. It was a memorable moment. We were both jumping with joy. It seemed that I was holding Murli and Ma and Papa as I hugged him.

"What are you doing here? I could never imagine you leaving Murli, and can't believe that I am seeing you here," I said to Raja in disbelief.

"I had to leave, it is a long story, but I had to leave Murli, Papa was not happy with me and we were not getting along well," he replied.

Raja had left Murli soon after I moved out from there and was looking for a job at the BPO. We were happy to have met each other after such a long time. We hugged again and the hug brought back all my childhood memories in a flash, the kites, the fields, the pond, the swim, the orchards, the fruits, the train, the races and Ma and Papa. Raja had an altercation with his father and had left our town in search of a job and an identity for himself. He was living with a distant relative in the outskirts of Gaulpur. Raja narrated his story in short and informed me that Ma and Papa were fine. I told him about my new job and how it was to be at the Mehta Mansion. He gave me his contact details and we promised to keep in touch and meet up soon. I still did not have any phone number where he could reach me so I gave him the address of Mehta Mansion instead.

We were delighted to have met by chance as Raja did not know about my whereabouts and hence was unable to let me know that he was in town. He was confident of getting this job at the NextEdge BPO. It was a job in their mailroom for despatching couriers to their clients and vendors. The salary was reasonable and Raja wanted to grab this job so that he could start earning at the earliest and prove his father wrong as he did not think him worth even a penny. He had met the Manager at the NextEdge BPO and his response seemed very positive though he had asked for some time to revert to Raja on the outcome of the interview. Raja was very hopeful of bagging this job. I was happy for him as I had never thought that Raja would ever work in his lifetime. It would be nice for him to get a job and start earning himself without having to depend on his father.

We were exchanging notes when Mehta Sir returned from the office. He looked at the two of us and then turned towards the car. I quickly opened the door for him and nodded at Raja bidding him goodbye. Raja waited for us to drive out of the parking lot and nodded in return to me as he stood there seeing us move out of the BPO complex. The sedan was rolling effortlessly on the road as I sat proudly behind the wheel. I was flying past vehicles and humming a tune in my mind. I was flowing with the sedan as it ran smoothly even at high speeds. My eye caught the needle of the speedometer that was continuously pushing itself towards the right and I realized I was speeding. I had pushed the accelerator too far in my excitement of having met my childhood friend. My foot had been pressing the accelerator unconsciously as I ran after the train at Murli in my dream. My thoughts were running at break neck speed and so was my foot. I noticed the speedometer just in time and took charge of myself and the sedan. It could have been fatal if I had not returned to reality in time. Split seconds can change destiny for people on the road. Another second could have seen us crashing into a truck that was right in front of us. I was headed for the truck as I was completely lost in my thoughts and I came back to my senses just in the nick of time. I released the accelerator softly and slowed down gradually and smiled as I was very happy to have met Raja and was lost in the thoughts of my childhood. My attention was diverted from my thoughts by Mehta Sir's crisp and loud voice which echoed in my ears like a wake up alarm to wake me up from my day dreaming. His voice took the shape of words after some moments as I got back to reality. I was fortunate that Mehta Sir was engrossed in his conversation with Prem making me escape his anger as he would have blasted me for speeding. I looked at him from the rear view mirror and was relieved to find him busy looking at his laptop screen. I brought myself back to the car and my focus back to the road. I realized that I had to drive safely and stop day dreaming while driving to avoid putting everyone's life in danger. I thanked God for saving us and thanked Mehta Sir's laptop for saving me from a scolding that day.

Mehta Sir and Prem had a lengthy discussion about their meeting at the NextEdge BPO on their way back home. Such discussions had Mehta Sir talking and Prem nodding his head regularly. Prem's contribution to a discussion was his regular nod and an occasional "Hmm". I do not like to hear other people's conversation but some voices are too loud to ignore and one cannot help but hear all that is being said. Mehta Sir's voice gained a good high pitch whenever he spoke in excitement and this was one of such instances. I got to hear about their meeting and all that was discussed with the NextEdge BPO Head. Mehta Sir was not too happy about the meeting and was vocal about his disappointment at the attitude of the NextEdge BPO Head. Mehta Sir's anguish and Prem's indifference to everything in life were in strange contrast to each other. We returned to the Mansion with a disgruntled Mehta Sir and an indifferent Prem.

My subsequent journeys were very similar though Mehta Sir did not always return disappointed from meetings in fact majority of his meetings left him satisfied and happy at the outcome. I was always the silent spectator to the entire proceedings that took the shape of a one sided conversation in the car with Mehta Sir summarizing the meetings and Prem sitting with his glum dejected face just like our cows back home at Murli who seem to be engaged in an in depth meditation as they chew the cud while they sit still in a pensive mood. I had named Prem as 'Prem The Cow' by then.

I got to learn a lot about Mehta Sir's business lines by being in the car. I always picked up business terms from the conversation and tried to learn something new each time I drove him around. I also learnt about his family from his conversation with Mrs. Mehta when the two of them travelled together. It was strange that they forgot that I was in the car and that I had ears as they would talk about a lot of personal issues and their investments and almost gave a detailed account of their wealth. I was surprised that they were talking about such confidential matters in the presence of a perfect stranger. I definitely was a perfect stranger as they did not know anything about me. They would completely forget that they were not alone in the car. There were times when I would feel insecure that someday I could be caught by goons and asked to part with information about the Mehtas at gun point. I disclosed this fear to Mani and he laughed it off. "Don't bother so much Suraj. I think you watch too much television. You sure are freaking out. Don't watch too many movies else your imagination will get freakier. You must be going crazy. Just try to ignore whatever you hear. I do the same," he tried to put my fears to rest by laughing at them. "But Mani, don't you think they should take more care when they know they are not alone. How can they trust anyone like that? I may be sincere but everybody is not as sincere. They can create problems for themselves," I argued with Mani. But Mani was unperturbed. "Don't drain your brain on such things Suraj. Just relax and sleep. Nothing is going to happen, what you are imagining is too farfetched and will not happen, you are just over reacting, just let it be, don't think about it, the more you think the worse you will feel and there is no need to worry about this so it is best to just forget about it," he said in a convincing tone. I believed him and thought that Mani had been there for long at Mehta Mansion and he must be right so I ignored my fears and closed this chapter for good. It was fortunate that nothing untoward has happened there till date due to this habit of the Mehtas.

*C*hapter 14

It was three months since I had moved to the servant quarters of Mehta Mansion. Life was exceptionally good to me. But this was not the aim I had set out with from Murli, my dreams were far beyond this lifestyle. I knew I would not be able to realize my dreams of making it big if I continued my job with Mehta Sir. I would contemplate about my future while I sat in the car waiting for Mehta Sir each day. The future was nebulous as I knew my goal but the path to my goal was still hazy. I was not here to spend my time waiting in the car doing nothing. My aim for coming to Gaulpur was very different. I knew I had to soon take a leap and move towards my goal. It was the month of August that year. Mrs. Mehta was taking a stroll in the morning and as she passed by me she said, "Suraj, you will make it big one day. I can see it! I know you will. You have the potential in you to make a fortune for yourself. I would like to be invited to the party you throw on your first success." I smiled and thanked her. "Don't forget to invite me to your wedding too, Suraj," she added. I smiled again and saw Anita standing behind her and knew that Anita was the girl I would marry. Anita smiled at me for the first time and left. My eyes kept chasing her till she was out of focus. I had to plan for my marriage soon and that brought a big question mark in front of my eyes.

I needed a house of my own before I could ask Anita and getting a home meant more money. "How do I get more money? I need to build a larger corpus of funds before I can speak to Anita." I kept talking to myself till I got into the driver's seat. My brain was jumbled up with a flurry of questions that remained unanswered. It resembled the heavy traffic on the roads of Gaulpur where vehicles were zooming past me from all sides. I was standing there like the traffic inspector making figures in the air with my moving arms in an aim to direct the traffic. The vehicles kept moving while I stood there stationary like a lamp post. I did not want to be stagnated as a driver for life. This is not what I had set out for from Murli. I had not left my home to be just a driver in Gaulpur. My dreams were big and larger than life and I had the will to achieve them but I was directionless at that point of time.

Anita had a dusky complexion and long black hair that curled up on her forehead to hide her deep brown eyes. Her eyes were very expressive and her smile was breathtaking. I had seldom seen her talk to other people in the Mansion. She was a reserved person who spoke mostly with her expressive eyes. Anita was an industrious worker who was known for her punctuality. She was like a companion and an assistant to Mrs. Mehta. She lived in an apartment close to Mehta Mansion. She did not have a family I was told. She had lost her parents in her childhood and was brought up by an aunt who too had passed away after some years. I later learnt that both her father and mother were school teachers. They had migrated from Dhuri to Gaulpur when Anita was an infant. Anita was the only child of her parents like me. Her parents' vocation had brought them to Gaulpur. They were both teaching at the Rose Petals School till they met with an accident while going on an excursion with their students. It must have been very traumatic for Anita to face this tragedy. Her aunt had decided to take care of Anita when her parents passed away. Anita had finished her schooling but did not go to college as her aunt could not afford it so Anita took up some long distance vocational courses instead. Her aunt had been diagnosed of cancer and succumbed to the disease after an year of suffering leaving Anita all alone in this big wide world. Anita was all alone in this world and that gave her more time to help Mrs. Mehta with great devotion. Mrs. Mehta and the rest of the staff always praised her and that somehow made me feel very proud. I do not know why I felt that way but maybe it was due to the fact that I had made a decision about marrying her. I thought about this with such confidence that I forgot to even ask her for her opinion about me and whether she was seeing someone else or not. I had taken a decision and was sure about her response. I was getting over confident about her.

Mani would sit with me after dinner and we spoke at length. We had got used to each other's company and there was a special bond that had developed between us making us the best of friends. Mani was the assistant that Mehta Sir trusted the most and perhaps this was the reason that he had been allocated a separate room at the servant quarters. He was always up to date about Mehta Sir's business as well as his whereabouts but did not disclose any information to anybody. Mani would talk at length about his family and his hometown Alsi. Alsi is a small industrial town about one hundred kilometers from

Gaulpur. The industries in this town are mainly of motor parts and leather goods. His wife made some money by helping a tailor at Alsi. He had two children who went to school. His son was eight and daughter six years old. His wife and children were living with his parents at Alsi. He would get emotional while he spoke about his family. His eyes had a spark in them when he spoke about his children. I would add my childhood experiences to his narrations. We were bonding very well. We would sit down together before dinner and exchange notes about the day. Life was moving at a comfortably smooth pace.

Anita paid special visits to the kitchen garden patch behind the dormitory to get Basil leaves in the evening. She would carefully select the leaves and pluck them softly. I had seen her at the patch several times but could not gather courage to speak to her. I wanted to let her know how I felt about her and about us but my words would get muted whenever I saw her. Her presence had me dumbstruck.

*C*hapter 15

It was an extraordinary evening. Mehta Sir was travelling to Devon. I was taking a stroll behind the dormitory when I heard soft footsteps approaching behind me and was delighted to see Anita walking towards the kitchen garden. She walked up to the Basil tree and I walked towards her.

"Do you like Basil leaves?" I asked her. "Yes, I like to take them with me for my morning tea. It keeps me healthy. Do you know it helps fight the germs, and you can only pluck them in daylight," she said with a smile. I smiled back and said, "Yes, I have heard about it." "I like my tea with Basil leaves. My mother always used basil leaves and ginger for our tea," she mentioned.

I stood there waiting for her to pluck the leaves. I was trying to gather some courage to speak to her but was not too successful in my attempt. I saw her pluck the leaves and as she was about to leave I managed to open my mouth to let some words out.

"I . . . . I wanted to ask you . . . . ask you . . . about your parents," I tried stating in a single breath as I did not want her to be reminded about her loss but could just manage completing the sentence with some hiccups.

"I lost them a long time back. I do not wish to talk about them Suraj else I will break down. I need to leave now else I will be late in reaching home," she said in a hurried tone.

"I am sorry. I did not want to hurt you at all. I apologize for what I said. I really am." I really did feel sorry and was angry with myself as I saw a tear in her eye. I had been stupid and insensitive in asking her such a touchy question. I had wanted to start a conversation but unfortunately picked up the wrong question in my nervousness. I was annoyed with myself for having such a bad start to a new relationship. "I can walk you home if it is ok with you," I asked her hesitatingly to make up for my stupidity. "I will manage, it is not too far," she smiled and looked away. "No, I insist, I will walk you back home," I said to Anita. "You do not have to Suraj. I know you want to apologize but it is ok. I am used to the question and honestly speaking, I am fine, please don't bother. Don't worry about me Suraj. I will be ok. Thanks anyways. I will leave now, I have to," she said to me and moved hurriedly towards the Mansion gate. I was surprised at how she had been able to read my mind and that made me feel great. It was not such a bad start after all. This was the first time she had spoken to me. I was thankful for the dormitory being close to the kitchen garden and also to Mehta Sir's absence from town which had given me this opportunity to talk to Anita. I wanted the conversation to last a little longer but could not think of anything to ask her. I was thinking hard and fast and suddenly came upon an idea to start a conversation with her.

"Anita, how do you select the basil leaves? I have seen you look at them closely before you pluck them but I cannot figure out what is it that you are looking for?" Anita smiled and said, "I look for bigger leaves that are soft and not too dark in colour. I avoid plucking smaller leaves." "Oh, now I know," I said to Anita. "I have to leave now," Anita responded and turned towards the main gate.

It must have been two minutes but they were like a rainfall in a desert. I held those two minutes in my palm like a prime possession and walked back to my dorm as I saw Anita returning to her home. I wanted to lock these two minutes in a treasure chest and hide the key in some secret place where no one could find it. I was mesmerized by her presence and dreamt of her that night. Life had suddenly become very beautiful, happy and full of hope. I was happy to have something to look forward to in my life and in Gaulpur. Life seemed to be showering happiness on me in abundance. The day was so different from my first day at Gaulpur. My life had changed so much since then.

Things are not always as smooth as one would expect and good times are followed by the not so good times in a cyclical manner. I could sense trouble brewing closer home. I had this special sense that made me foresee things. When I say foresee I do not mean see them as they would happen or pin point to the exact thing but it is just a feeling that something good or bad is coming up soon. And of course it is generally something bad most of the times. I was uneasy at this sense that was prevailing around me telling me to beware of what the future might unfold.

Chapter 16

Mehta Sir's son Aditya was arriving from Sweden and I was to bring him home from the airport. Mrs. Mehta was very excited that her son was returning home after an year. She had the whole house repainted and got it decorated with flowers and lights. She went to the temple early in the morning. I could hear her continuously passing instructions to the servants all through the day. Mehta Mansion was glittering with lights and joy and Mrs. Mehta had never been this happy before. Mrs. Mehta's smile was warm and infectious and it made her wrinkles disappear each time she smiled. Her gait had got a touch of excitement that she could not hide at all.

Mehta Sir asked me to be ready at 11 p.m. to leave for the airport. He was exceptionally quiet during the forty minutes drive to the airport. The silence in the car was sharper than the silence of the night. Aditya walked out of the airport and got into the car while Mehta Sir sat there staring at him. They shared a hello as though they were being introduced to each other for the first time. It was not like a father son reunion at all leaving me both confused and surprised. I was waiting for them to hug each other and share a joke or two and laugh like Papa and I do when we meet after a gap of some days but here it was a very different situation. There were no hugs and no exchange of pleasant notes. I felt uncomfortable and uneasy at the situation. It appeared as though the top leaders of two warring countries had been forced to share a podium.

Mehta Sir and Aditya argued throughout the journey from the airport to Mehta Mansion. I could not understand the reason for the argument but I sensed that it did have a serious background. The forty minutes ride from the airport to the Mansion was like a volcanic eruption in the making. It seemed like an explosion could happen any minute now. Both Mehta Sir and Aditya kept repeating their statements without any one of them agreeing to the other's point of view. They were like two trains running parallel to each other at different speeds and moving towards different destinations. There was no consensus in their thought process making them sound like stubborn children who were bent upon proving the other wrong. They were both talking to themselves and not to each other as neither of them tried to listen to the other. It was a cacophony that no one was paying any attention to. I was a mere spectator to the growing noise which was a premonition of the troubled times to come.

The car was filled with the negativity of the argument when we reached Mehta Mansion. I had never felt so claustrophobic in my life before. I wanted to jump out of the car as soon as I could. I thanked God when we entered the gates to the Mansion. I parked the car in the porch and jumped out of my seat and opened the door for Mehta Sir and Aditya. There was a bitter and uneasy silence that emerged out of the car with Aditya and Mehta Sir. I walked through the layers of unease that surrounded the car to reach the boot. I pulled out Aditya's bags from the boot and placed them near the main entrance. "Aditya, my son, you are back," Mrs. Mehta's sweet voice pierced through the bitterness as she came and hugged Aditya. She was in tears as she hugged Aditya. Her tears said so much about her happiness, her endless wait to meet her son, her hope that she would not have to say goodbye to her son again and her immense love for her son. I thought about my mother and became emotional for a while. Aditya hugged her but this hug too was not warm and I could sense some distance in this mother son relationship too. I wondered if the rich people lacked emotions or found it difficult to express their love openly. I was unable to understand this behavior and looked at the three of them in a confused state of mind.

"Aditya, I have cooked myself today. I have made your favourite dishes. Take a shower and join us at the dinner table. We have so much to talk. Let us go inside," Mrs. Mehta said in a loving tone to Aditya. She held Aditya's hand and took him inside the Mansion.

The darkness of the night seemed lighter than the darkness of the bitterness I had sensed at that time. Mrs. Mehta's appearance had helped dissipate the negativity to some extent though the son and father had walked in different directions while they headed towards the main door of their home. Mehta Sir asked me to take Aditya's bags inside Mehta Mansion. This was the first time I was allowed inside the Mansion. The bags were so heavy that I had to literally crawl with them into the Mansion. I was reminded of my stay at the railway platform where I helped passengers with their luggage. I had one bag on my head and I was pulling the other while I dragged myself into the Mansion. It was an ordeal to get the bags inside the Mansion.

The Mansion was splendor and royalty personified. I was in a wonderland and felt like a King walking through the Mansion. The smallest of things was of ultra superior taste and it was a palatial setup inside the Mansion. The golden edges of the red curtains swayed and turned into a spiral with the wind. The doors had carved brass and bronze embellishments on them. Each piece of furniture was a true work of art with extremely expensive upholstery. The carvings on the furniture were very intricate and had a story to narrate. The tables of walnut wood had beautiful maple leaves carved on them. The paintings and murals displayed on the walls were masterpieces of renowned painters. The chandeliers and crystal were breathtaking. The China Cabinets had on display the most exquisite chinaware with twenty four carat gold polish. Each corner had a statue that spoke about the richness and luxury of Mehta Mansion. The banisters of the stairway were carved with animal figures. The pure white marble floor had brass grouting that was shining spotlessly. A stream of water ran down one of the walls like a waterfall into a fountain base on one side of the hallway. The arch of the hallway had marble and granite murals with semi precious stones etched in them. There were wooden pillars in the hallway that had elephant carvings on them. The main hall had marble pillars with elephants and deer carvings. The carpets were silk on silk and had unique and extraordinary motifs woven on them. The window panes were of stained glass to lend coloured light into all the rooms. I walked up some steps when I saw an open door that led to the guest bathroom. The jacuzzi looked so inviting that I started to imagine myself in the jacuzzi with soft music playing in the backdrop. I was humming a tune and floating in the glorious ambience when something brought me back to reality.

Chapter 17

I heard somebody shout and I saw Mani and Naval rush out from the interior of the Mansion. There was a commotion and I could not comprehend what was happening around me. Two more servants came running out and rushed out of the house to the main gate. Mani gestured to me to leave the Mansion as he ran out of the hallway. I slipped out of the Mansion with a heavy heart as my tour of the grand palace had been sadly interrupted. But there was something wrong and unusual about the chaotic activity inside the Mansion. I had to wait to get an update from Mani. I walked out of the main hall and inched towards the dorm thinking about the course of events that had taken place that day. There was a joyous ambience at the Mansion in the morning that had taken an ugly turn towards the evening and now suddenly there seemed to be some untoward happening at the Mansion that had swept out its happiness in just one stroke.

Naval was the main cook at Mehta Mansion. Naval was a tall man with a long pointed nose, long fingers and a moustache that stood on his lip like a bird spreading its wings and ready to take a flight. He had a reputation for cooking the most delicious meals though his appearance was more like that of an Army Chief. Naval, Mani and I got along well. We did not have much in common but we were able to connect very well. Naval and Mani were card buddies and played cards till midnight every day without fail. I preferred to sleep early so that I sleep today and get up tomorrow. Naval and Mani teased me for sleeping for long hours. I needed my sleep else I could not drive comfortably. It was rare for Mehta Sir to move out at night so we would return to the Mansion latest by nine at night. I usually slept by ten thirty and got up at four in the morning as I had to take Mehta Sir for Golf. Mehta Sir was a keen golfer and did not skip it even for a day. We carried his golf bag with us even when we drove out of town. We left for the Golf Course at five every morning and were back by six thirty. The Golf Course was lush green with a beautiful and serene landscape that transported me to a different world altogether. I would walk in the parking lot and admire the Golf Course from a distance. At times I would chat with the other drivers with whom I had got acquainted at the Golf Course. Some of their masters were very regular just like Mehta Sir but many did not visit the Golf Course as frequently. It was a fifty minutes wait at the parking lot while Mehta Sir played with his friends. These fifty minutes made me restless as my mind would start questioning me about my future and my goals in life. I used to walk around the parking lot thinking about my future and how I would reach my goals.

Mani's face was a canvas painted with a plethora of emotions when he returned from the Mansion. I was unable to decipher what was going through his mind as he sat down with his pack of cards that lay like defeated warriors on the table. He was too silent and his pensive mood worried me. His hands shuffled the cards nervously. The cards slipped from his hand and collapsed on the table. I wanted to give him time to calm down before I could ask him about what had happened inside the Mansion that evening. Mani's silence had become so intense that it was shouting in search of a vent to find some respite. I kept staring at Mani and his growing tension. We were both so quite that we could hear our hearts beating at erratic rates. I was waiting for Mani to open up while Mani planned to keep his tension to himself. It was a very long wait till Mani mumbled "Hmm . . . ," and that was followed by another silent pause. It took Mani another twenty minutes to take the decision to confide in me.

Aditya had shot one of his friends and they had to rush him to the hospital. Aditya, I learnt, was notorious for losing his temper and getting into brawls. He was very different from Mehta Sir and Mrs. Mehta. He had unfortunately not inherited any of the positive traits from his parents. He was not in agreement with the way Mehta Sir was running his businesses and Mehta Sir was not appreciative of Aditya's approach towards business. Aditya had the arrogance that power and wealth can bring and an anger that comes from seeing disagreement about your views, choices and opinion. Aditya was what one would call a 'spoilt brat'. He had been born with a platinum spoon in his mouth and wealth and power had come to him by virtue of his birth making him too arrogant with a foul temper and an over inflated ego. He wanted to have his will and way in every little thing in life. He was rude and spat venom each time he spoke to the servants. I could visualize him as a serpent raising its hood and getting ready to bite anyone who tried crossing his way. He was very handsome in his appearance but his mannerisms made him look like the ugliest creature on the face of mother Earth. He was like an ugly dog that snapped at anyone who passed by him.

Aditya's friend was fortunately alive and out of danger. We were not sure why Aditya had fought with his friend. Neither did we get to know what prompted Aditya to shoot his friend. I heard Lakhan comment the next morning, "It is unfortunate that anger can take over a man's senses and make him do senseless things". Lakhan was so right. There cannot be any sensible reason in shooting somebody. We saw some police jeeps parked at the porch till late night. There were some people who came down to meet Mehta Sir. There was a hushed silence and then things seemed to get normal in a couple of days.

Aditya had returned with a mission. He wanted Mehta Sir to close down one of the businesses as it was not as profitable as expected. He wanted to use that factory space for setting up a mall. Malls meant big business but Mehta Sir did not want to displace his factory staff and venture into a new territory. This led to a second round of argument between Mehta Sir and Aditya. Then such altercations became a routine and Mehta Mansion was abuzz with daily news of quarrels. Mehta Mansion was losing its peace. The mornings at Mehta Mansion were not as cheerful as they had been some months ago. And the nights too did not have the peace and comfort that we had become accustomed to. The air of Mehta Mansion was getting uneasy with the discomfort of the father and son disagreements. Mehta Sir had even become irregular for his Golf.

It was a respite when Aditya was away from the Mansion. He would move out to meet his friends or go on business or personal trips often giving the Mansion a breathing space. I preferred the Mansion without Aditya and I am sure so did the others. His absence was a boon to all. The Mansion had a touch of serenity and peace when Aditya was away. We feared his return as that brought an evil whiff of air with it.

Chapter 18

It was the month of November that year. The day was unusually cold and the weather had the worst dullness that I had ever seen in my life. Life was moving at a snail's pace as a premonition of the times to come. I had taken Mehta Sir for a short trip out of the town and we returned in the afternoon. I walked to the kitchen for lunch where I met Mani and Naval. The three of us sat together for lunch and decided to go out to see a football match the next afternoon. The stadium was close by so we would need half a day's leave. We were hesitant in asking for half day's leave from Mehta Sir. He would have definitely not liked to see three of his men disappear together. We coaxed Mani into asking Mehta Sir for the favour. Mani was nervous and hesitant in approaching Mehta Sir for the half day leave for the three of us. Mehta Sir looked at Mani with an indifferent look, just like the look that Prem usually had fixed on his melancholy face. Mehta Sir seemed lost in his thoughts so he kept staring at Mani. There was a long pause and Mehta Sir retraced from his thoughts and asked Mani why the three of us wanted to go out together. Mani told him about the football match nervously. "Football Match? So, . . . you guys plan to go to the football match tomorrow afternoon," exclaimed Mehta Sir. "I can let the three of you go but you need to take me with you too," Mehta Sir said with a soft smile on his face. That came as a pleasant surprise from him. The three of us were overjoyed. The next morning woke us up earlier than usual as we were unable to contain our excitement. We anxiously waited for the afternoon to go to the stadium. It was a great day and Mehta Sir was also accompanying us. We were a little nervous too as Mehta Sir would be with us at the stadium and we were not sure if we could feel comfortable in his presence. Three of us were soon seated in the sedan for our trip to the stadium with Mehta Sir. Mehta Sir had his white hat on as he sat like a child in the sedan. He was impatiently looking at his watch and tapping it every five minutes to see if it was working or not. He seemed to be making time run faster for him. He could not wait to reach the stadium. We were able to get good seats, all thanks to Mehta Sir. He was extremely influential and his reputation reached everywhere even before he did. People at the stadium greeted him and gave us the best seats. We were the special guests of the match promoters that day and had a gala time. Mehta Sir was like a teenager that afternoon as he cheered the local team with full gusto. Our fears of having him around were soon wiped out. He treated us to colas and snacks and recalled how he had played football in college. He was a very different person that evening, so alive and energetic like we had never seen him before. He would jump up with joy at every goal and his jaw dropped seeing the goalkeeper tripping or missing the goal. He was living in his glorious past and reliving its charm through the match. He must have had a great childhood and youth. He spoke about the matches he had played at school and college while we returned from the stadium. He remembered the exact number of goals made by him in each and every match that he had played in his life time. He definitely had a very sharp memory. We were listening intently to the narrative of his adventurous life. This was a different Mehta Sir, very different from the one we had known till now. He was not at all acting like our Boss that day. He was like any one of us. His reminiscence of his past made him smile and his eyes seemed to be watching everything all over again. We were enjoying every bit of the day with him. I drove into the Mansion and parked the sedan at the porch. Mehta Sir got off the sedan followed by the three of us. He was humming some tune while he went inside. Mani and I returned to our dorm while Naval walked towards the kitchen at the Mansion. It had been a very pleasant evening. Mani, Naval and I kept discussing Mehta Sir till late in the night. We were intrigued to see him the way he was at the stadium. It was a nice fun filled day. I slept soundly and was up early next morning to take Mehta Sir to the Golf Course.

Chapter 19

It was close to Diwali, the Festival of Lights, and I wanted to go home to meet my parents so I asked Mehta Sir for a two week's holiday and he agreed. I thanked him and set off to shop for gifts for my parents. I had to get them good gifts for Diwali. I was ready early morning. The train was to leave at five. I would miss seeing Anita and that made me feel a bit low. I was out of my dormitory at 3:30 a.m. and took a bus to the railway station. I met Sundar at the station who recognized me instantly. "You seem to have put on some weight," he said. "Yes, I get good food and good sleep every day and it has started to show on me," I smiled. He was overjoyed to see me after so many months. I could see a good friend in him. He treated me with a free Buntea from his tea stall. He also gave me some bags of chips for my journey. I was very touched by the gesture and felt cared for. The platform brought back many memories of my first fortnight at Gaulpur. Some vendors recognized me and waved to me. I waved back and we exchanged greetings before I boarded my train.

The journey was exciting as I was going to meet Ma and Papa after some months. The train slowly slugged and moved out of the Gaulpur station. I could not wait for Murli to come. My eyes kept going back to my wrist watch every minute. Time was moving too slowly. I was planning all that I had to do during this fortnight at home. I hung to my bag like one would hold a treasure. I did not want to lose it as it had gifts for Ma and Papa. There was a lot to be done and I had very little time with me. I was wishing for forty eight hours in a day. I jumped out of the train at the sight of Murli. I had become an expert in jumping in and out of trains due to my stay at the railway platform. I walked out of the platform and ran to my home shouting Ma Papa Ma Papa Ma Papa. I could not contain my emotions on being home after so many months. I was finally home!!

It was a memorable Diwali as Ma and Papa were overjoyed to see me and we celebrated the festival in a lavish style. Ma and Papa were happy that I had a good job. They wanted to know about the Mehtas and the Mehta Mansion and my dormitory. They listened to my entire list of escapades at Gaulpur. I narrated the story of my stay at the railway platform and how I met Mehta Sir. They were intrigued and fascinated with the description of Mehta Mansion. Ma's worries about my house were also over as I had a decent place to sleep at Mehta Mansion. I made them visualize the dormitory and our kitchen at the servant quarters at Mehta Mansion and they were happy that I was comfortably placed in Gaulpur. They were anxious to know about the cars I was driving and how the other servants got along with me. They were also keen to know how was Mehta Sir as a person. We spoke at length and Ma and Papa were thoroughly engrossed in the conversation. They wanted to know every detail so I took time to explain every little thing to them. They seemed to be living through my life with me as I walked them through its details. They had a lot of questions that they kept asking me about my job throughout my two week stay at Murli. I too was over excited and kept them occupied with my narrative of the city of Gaulpur, the Mehta Mansion, the Mehtas and the servants, et al. I told them I would be calling them to Gaulpur soon. Murli was in a celebration mood with lights, decorations and the earthen *diya* lamps defining the festivity at every house. Ma and Papa kept showering their blessings on me on seeing the gifts. I wanted to spend the entire vacation with them. Raja had also returned home for Diwali. Raja and I painted my house in a day. Ours hands were aching with the long strokes of the paint brush by the end of the day. My biceps were hurting by the time I hit my bed but the satisfaction of doing up my home myself was immense. I slept well after a long and tiresome but a productive day. Next day we painted Raja's house. Raja's father was very happy to know that his son was employed and doing well for himself.

We planned to visit all our friends and relatives and borrowed Raja's car for two days. We drove all around Murli, Devon and Jhilmil. Nana and Nani were overjoyed and had a sense of gratification seeing us after a long time. We spent an entire day with them. Ma and Nani cooked a delicious meal for us while Papa, Nana and I took a walk near the lake. It was a wonderful experience to be surrounded by my family. These memories were a priceless treasure I was taking back with me to Gaulpur.

My Nani teased me as usual about getting me married to her neighbour's granddaughter. "She is a nice girl Suraj. Why don't you meet her? Let me call her here," she said. "No, Nani, you don't have to. I will let you know when to call her but not now", I pleaded. She seemed very adamant and was trying to force her decision on me. I was a little hesitant in mentioning Anita but Nani was too assertive so I let the cat out. "Nani, Nana, Ma and Papa, you need to know this, there is this girl in Gaulpur, her name is Anita and I think she will be a better wife than this girl Nani is suggesting," I said with a straight face and had the four of them staring at me with their jaws dropped. "She is really nice, why are you all staring at me like that. You have all been talking about my marriage and now that I am ready for it and have saved you the trouble of finding a girl for me, don't you think you should be happy for me," I continued as they looked at me totally surprised. Ma asked, "Suraj, why did'nt you tell us about her before? Why were you waiting to be asked?" "So I have told you now. Is it not ok? I was going to tell you eventually," I said softly. "When would you have told us? After marrying her? We would like to meet her at least and get to know her?" Papa said to me while Ma, Nana and Nani smiled. I could tell they were all very happy for me. Nani smiled and said, "Ok then she must be better than our neighbour's granddaughter I am sure and since you like her, I am fine. Can't just wait to be at your wedding. I will make her wedding dress with my own hands," she said with tears in her eyes. I hugged Nani and then Nana and Ma and Papa and we rejoiced at the news. I ran to the market to get *samosas* and *jalebis* from Guptajee for us to celebrate. I was mentally at peace with myself after telling them about Anita. I was happy that my family was supportive of my decision and that filled those moments with delight. We left early morning from Jhilmil the next day and were back in Murli. Ma tried to ask me about Anita's background and I realized how little I knew about her. I told Ma the little bit I knew about Anita while she listened with a sweet smile on her happy and satisfied face. She was very supportive of my decision and seemed to be very happy about it too.

Next day was Dusshera, the festival of the victory of truth and righteousness over evil. Ma, Papa, Raja, Raja's sister and parents accompanied me to the stage near Sinda Talaab where the local teenagers had organzised the *Ramleela* and *Dussehra* celebrations. It was a very engrossing *Ramleela* followed by the burning of the effigy of Ravan. My dreams floated in front of my eyes as I saw the ten headed Ravan being killed. I wanted to kill the Ravan within me, my own Ravan, my laziness and my contentment as I had to move ahead in life and follow my dreams. The smoke built up around us and my dreams were also covered in smog as I was still not able to see the road to my dreams. What next, when, where and how were the repetitive questions that my mind put across to me and I could not seek immediate and instant answers to them. My mind kept harping for an answer and I was unable to respond to it.

The fortnight was too short and got over in no time. It was soon time to return to Gaulpur and to Mehta Mansion and of course to Anita. I packed my bag with reluctance and took off for Gaulpur. I was unhappy to be leaving Ma and Papa but looked forward to meeting Anita soon. The thought of meeting Anita brought a smile back on my face and the unhappiness seemed to fade away instantly. I had something to look forward to in life now. Ma had given me a green silk sari for Anita. I was thinking how would I give it to her. "She may get offended and not take it and probably misunderstand me," I said to myself. I thought of keeping it with me till the right moment when I pop the question to her and can give it as a gift or a blessing from my parents.

I was back at Mehta Mansion late in the evening and to my job and my dorm and of course to Anita. I got out of the vacation mood and was back in form for my job. Mani was happy to see me at the dorm. I had got a shirt for him which eventually became his favourite shirt as it was just the right size for him and made his paunch look smaller than what it was.

Chapter 20

Some days later I had to take Mrs. Mehta to her sister's place at Dori, a two hour drive from Mehta Mansion. Mehta Sir was travelling abroad and Mrs. Mehta's driver had fallen ill. So I was asked to drive Mrs. Mehta to Dori. I jumped up with joy when I learnt I had to drive Mrs. Mehta and Anita to Dori. It was a dream come true. I just could not believe myself that I would be able to see Anita throughout the day. I could not sleep in anticipation of the next morning and the joy that it would be bringing in its wake for me. I kept staring out of the window waiting to welcome the morning sky and the wait seemed endless as dawn took its own sweet time to make an appearance. I jumped out of my bed the moment I heard a bird chirp and dashed towards the washroom. I was ready within fifteen minutes and ran to the garage to get the car to the porch. I was pacing up and down the porch waiting for my esteemed passengers to appear from the interiors of the Mansion. I could not help letting out my broad toothpaste advertisement smile when I saw Anita coming out from the main door. It was a dream walking towards me at that moment. Anita looked very charming in her peach dress. Her eyes held my world in them as she smiled at me. I wanted to hold that moment in time forever. I wanted the clocks of the world to stop ticking so that my dream could continue without any interruption till eternity. I wanted to order time to stop there and then.

I suddenly heard a thud as Mani walked past and slapped my shoulder. I realized my time had moved ahead and so did my moment that I was beholding bringing my dream to an end. I looked around and saw Mrs. Mehta standing next to the car. Anita was standing beside her. Mrs. Mehta and Anita were soon seated in the car while one of the servants Gangu loaded the car with the gifts that Mrs. Mehta was taking for her sister and her family. I put my grey bag in the boot and my water bottle in the slot of my car door. Mrs. Mehta asked Gangu to keep the snack and fruit basket in front near my seat. A water dispenser and disposable glasses were also placed on the seat next to mine.

We were soon ready to leave. It was like a dream come true as I would be with Anita throughout the day and that made me look forward to the day with all happiness. The three of us soon set off to Dori in our sedan. The road to Dori was very narrow and had less traffic than in the city. The road was lined with eucalyptus trees on both sides. I could see some honeybee farms where villagers were breeding honeybees for their honey at a distance from the road. There were small shops on the roadside where some villagers had put up honey stalls. Mrs. Mehta asked me to stop at one of the stalls and buy four bottles of honey. I bought one bottle for my mother too. Ma is very fond of honey and this honey was in its purest form, right out of the honeybee farm. I knew she would love to have this honey in her tea. Further on our route we drove past some brick kilns. The smoke from the kilns had a strange smell, the smell of earth, bricks, terracota and creativity. I watched the smoke rise and make designs in the sky. It reminded me of the goods train at Murli. I tried not to drift away into my dream land and with Anita being around I could not waste those precious moments in my normal day dreaming. I took charge of myself and focused on the road in front and Anita through the rear view mirror. It was an enjoyable journey on the whole. The weather, traffic, landscape, fields, trees, plantations and my company were all in a good mood and that made everything so special. It was like going on a full day picnic with my beloved.

A few tractors and small trucks were the only vehicles we met on our way to Dori. It was a weekday so the traffic was very less compared to the weekends. We drove past some more villages on our way. The hutments and fields reminded me of Murli. The fields looked yellow from a distance so I assumed them to be mustard fields. Mrs. Mehta asked me inquisitively, "Are there similar fields in Murli, Suraj?" "Yes Ma'am, we have sugarcane fields back home, there are'nt any *sarson* fields there though. My father and I have sugarcane fields back home in Murli that we survive on. I meant I was working at the fields when I was at Murli. Now my father is working there alone with some help from the village. We sell our harvest at Devon at the auction at the sugar mills. My father and I drive down to Devon with the harvest each year but this year my father had to go on his own with a cousin of his." Mrs. Mehta sensed how I must be missing home so she said, "I know it is not easy to be away from home. But we have to lose some to gain some. And of course you are doing very well for yourself. Your parents must be proud of you. I would like to meet them whenever they are in town next."

I nodded and looked at Anita from the side view mirror. She was lost in her thoughts and was nodding too. I knew she was thinking about her parents so I tried to divert her attention from her thoughts. "Anita, have you ever seen the sugarcane fields?" I asked her. "No, I have not, but I would like to see them one day." I was glad I could change her focus from her thoughts. "Yes I will take you to Murli soon and show you the sugarcane fields," I thought to myself. "Yes, and the sugarcane juice is to die for Anita. It is very delicious. I like to eat the sugarcane too. You must try the sugarcane juice with some mint," I tried to move her away from her thoughts and was successful in my attempt. She nodded again and smiled.

We had left the Mansion at six in the morning and entered Dori at seven forty five, in less than two hours. The journey was super special and I felt I was driving through the clouds to the rainbow. Anita was definitely my rainbow with all the colours of joy that life could offer. We reached Mrs. Mehta's sister's villa by eight. I waited in the car while Mrs. Mehta and Anita walked through the courtyard into Kapoor Villa. I stepped out of the car after sometime and walked into the courtyard of Kapoor Villa. It was a beautiful villa that overlooked the hills that lined the skyline in front. It was a dreamy and cold morning. The sun was hiding behind the clouds making it a cool day. I was admiring the guava tree when one of the servants called me inside for breakfast. I was pampered with a rich breakfast of *aloo, pooris, boondi raita* and *halwa*. I thoroughly relished the delicacies. "This mango pickle is too spicy and is just the right recipe that Ma makes for me," I told the servant who was serving me. Mrs. Kapoor was passing by and smiled at me, "I am happy that you liked the pickle. I have made it myself. Don't feel shy, eat well, you have driven a long distance," she said. I was not at all shy as I did not even keep count of the *pooris* that I had gulped. The food was extraordinarily delicious and I enjoyed every bite of it. I had stuffed myself so much that I felt drowsy and was unable to keep my eyes open. I was almost asleep when Anita woke me up. I opened my eyes to the sight of two beautiful eyes staring at me. The light from the door brought sparkles in Anita's dreamy eyes. I thought I was in my dreamland but Anita brought me back to the world by calling out my name again. She was asking me to wake up and get ready to take Mrs. Mehta to the temple. It was such a nice feeling to be woken up by the love of my life. She informed me that we had to go to the temple. I washed my eyes and my face to freshen up to drive Mrs. Mehta and Anita to the temple.

Mrs. Mehta had earlier mentioned during the morning that she wanted to visit the Durga temple at Dori but it had slipped my mind. She and Anita hopped into the car while I drove them to the temple. It was a mile from the villa. Mrs. Mehta got off the car and walked towards the temple. Anita followed her and returned after ten minutes. Mrs. Mehta was still inside the temple doing the *parikrama*. I could see her walk around the temple from where I was standing. She must have gone around the temple at least eleven times in *parikrama*. We were waiting for Mrs. Mehta when a priest walked past our car. He turned around to look at us as though we had landed there from an alien world. He kept staring at us for some time and then he walked towards us. He raised his hand to bless us, "I can see that God will unite you as a couple very soon." Anita and I were taken aback and looked at each other and then at the priest. The priest smiled and walked away while Anita and I pretended that we had not heard anything. We felt a bit uneasy hearing the priest but somewhere in my heart I could hear a bell chiming that wanted the priest's blessing to come true. The chime was growing louder as I stood there with Anita by my side. My heart was singing praises for the priest and thanking him immensely. Anita kept looking at the temple and ignored my presence completely after the incident. Mrs. Mehta returned from the temple after ten minutes and gave us coconut and *mishri prashad*. "Don't you want to see *Durga Maa*?" she asked me. "Sure, I said, I had completely forgotten that I had to seek her blessings too, I will be back in five minutes," I said and ran up the steps to the main idol at the temple. I thanked *Durga Maa* as I had heard the best news of my life here. I also asked her for her blessings for helping me grow in my career. I did an extra *parikrama* of the temple to make *Durga Maa* happy and make my wish come true. We drove back to Kapoor Villa where we again had a rich and sumptuous lunch of *chole, bhature, shahi paneer, dum aloo, ghia raita* and *kheer*. I overate in my joy. I had eaten so much that I could not even breathe. I was in seventh heaven and was wishing the priest's prophecy to come true. I did not want the day to end at all. It was a beautiful and enchanting day that had kept me smiling throughout. I was at peace with myself and that made the day very special and important. Happiness can make the world look really very beautiful.

We left from Dori at about four in the evening. Anita did not look at me throughout our return journey. She pretended to be missing from the car. I tried to look at her from the rear view mirror but she kept peeping out of the window. She did not look unhappy due to the incident at the temple in the morning but ignored me. I could not catch her eye as she hid her face from me. She was trying to show indifference to the whole episode but I could tell she was not negatively bothered by it and that gave me all the hope that I wanted in life. I could see a ray of hope, my ray of hope in this indifference. I was unable to contain my excitement and had a beaming smile on my face through the entire week. We were home at six in the evening. Anita got off the car, glanced at me and grabbed her handbag before she walked into the Mansion with Mrs. Mehta. Mrs. Mehta got off the car and handed me a jar of pickle that she had got from her sister's house. "This is for you and only for you, don't share it with the others, my sister told me you had liked it and packed it for you" she chuckled. "That was very thoughtful of Ma'am, I really appreciate the gesture. Please thank her on my behalf," I thanked her and drove the car to the garage. It was indeed very thoughtful and nice of Mrs. Kapoor to have packed the pickle jar for me. She was as kind and generous as her sister Mrs. Mehta. Gangu unloaded the car. I took my belongings from the boot and kept the pickle jar in my grey bag. I was thanking Mehta Sir for being out station and Mrs. Mehta's driver who had fallen ill making way for the trip to be designed as per my wishes. "No, this trip was designed by God, and by His Wish," I told myself. "Hope we can go on many more such trips God," I sent a request to God. I called out to God to make the priest's prophecy come true. I walked to my dorm rejoicing at the prophecy. I entered the dorm humming and Mani looked at me with keen interest and moved his chin up asking me the reason for my delight. I smiled at him and gestured that it was nothing. "Did they feed you marijuana at Dori?" he asked. "No Mani, they fed me love!" I responded with a beaming smile. His left eyebrow went up questioningly and he kept staring at me. I ignored him as I was in another world. "How about some dinner Suraj?" asked Mani. "I am not hungry at all, had a week's fill at Dori," I said shaking my head and jumped into my bed and dozed off.

I saw the priest in my dreams and his prophecy kept echoing in my ears for weeks at length. And Anita showed me her indifference for a week and then seemed to have forgotten about it completely and was her normal self once again.

$\mathcal{C}$hapter 21

Life was moving at its regular pace. January ushered in a cold breeze and fog. It was the coldest winter of my lifetime. I bought myself a woollen cardigan and a fleece blanket from my savings. I preferred to drive Mehta Sir all day as the sedan had a good heating system that kept me warm and cozy. It was a nightmare to step out in the cold. I literally ran from the garage wing to the dorm to save myself from getting a frost bite. The cold breeze slapped my face with all its might and the tip of my nose turned red with the dropping temperature. We kept the doors and windows of the dorm tightly closed as the slightest of breeze was enough to freeze us. The cold weather brought dullness with it and some shocking news was to unfold soon. I was unaware of the shock that lay in store for me in the days to follow. Life was moving slowly and the days had lost their sheen with the sun having gone into hiding and fog taking over the morning sky. The fog hid from us everything that was there in sight. We were shocked to get the news in the morning. Mani came running to wake me up. We were not prepared to hear such news.

Mehta Sir was no more! We were hit by this shocking news in the morning. Mehta Sir had passed away in his sleep. I ran to the Mansion. The Mansion was flooded by relatives, friends, visitors, staff and the media. I went up to the hall where Mehta Sir's body had been kept. He looked so calm as though he was sleeping peacefully. I could not believe that he would never wake up now. He was gone away forever and far away from this world and its worries. I stood there for a while in tears and then saw Mrs. Mehta who was sitting next to his body. I offered my condolences to her. She nodded her head as she was not in a position to talk at all. We had to soon leave for the funeral. Mrs. Mehta wanted me to drive her. She slowly walked up to the car with Anita. I held the car door for the two ladies to get inside. Aditya followed them and sat in front. I waited for Aditya to tell me when to start. Aditya had second thoughts and he moved out of the car and turned to speak to Mrs. Mehta. "Mama, I will go with Dad," he said. Mrs. Mehta nodded as Aditya walked towards the hearse in which Mehta Sir was to be taken to the funeral ground. We waited for the hearse to leave and followed it. I drove Mrs. Mehta and Anita to the funeral ground. Mrs. Mehta was trying to keep her compose but I could tell from her expressions how much she was grieving. Her eyes had tears which could not be seen but felt. She was broken and shattered and still trying to keep calm as she faced the media and her relatives and friends. Her grief was building within her. I wanted to be by her side but she was surrounded by her relatives. Anita stood with her. Anita was also in pain but she was trying to look normal as she spoke to Mrs. Mehta. We came back to the Mehta Mansion after the funeral. The car was refusing to move without Mehta Sir. I found it difficult to drive as my limbs were giving away and I just could not take charge of my faculties. It was a traumatic experience that left me shaken from within. I stood there at the funeral and watched the smoke of the pyre rise. The view was all hazy through the smoke. We were all in tears as we saw a life going through the last ritual of this world. I could feel Mehta Sir's soul moving away from us forever. Two weeks of mourning slipped into a dull phase of some months of inactivity. An uncanny silence gripped Mehta Mansion.

I would sit in the porch and remember the time I drove Mehta Sir around the city. All my memories from the time I met Mehta Sir flashed back in front of my eyes as I sat there remembering Mehta Sir. My memory of my first meeting with Mehta Sir was absolutely fresh in my mind. The halo of his ring flashed in front of my eyes as I recollected how he had stood there waiting for his driver at the foot of the staircase when I met him for the first time. I still could not believe that he was not with us anymore. It was at this porch that he had offered me the first job of my life. It was at this very porch that I had waited for him every morning. I had spent hours driving him around every day. I thought about the football match where he had joined us and enjoyed watching the match like a teenager. I was reminded of the daily trips to the Golf Course. It seemed he would come back soon and I would wake up from my dream and take him for a drive. But this did not happen. It was not easy to come to terms with reality. I had formed a bond with Mehta Sir, a silent bond that had grown between us as we accompanied each other every day. He had always been very kind to me and treated me like his son. It was a big loss for me and I was not prepared to handle it. I had lost my Godfather.

We did not see Mrs. Mehta as often as we were used to seeing her. Anita was with Mrs. Mehta, trying to console her and help her face reality. I did not have much work to do now. Mrs. Mehta would ask me to drive her to the temple at times and to her relatives in the nearby city.

Anita would accompany her each time and seeing her brought joy and contentment in my life. Her presence itself would turn my ordinary life into an extraordinary one.

Joy and Polly were also very quiet and listless. They would walk around in the garden with Rocky but did not have the spark in their eyes that used to come from Mehta Sir's presence. They were grief stricken. Their tails were not wagging with joy anymore. I did not hear them bark for weeks at length. They sat at Mrs. Mehta's feet just like two bags of flesh and blood. Lakhan's scissors were not doing the regular waltz as the garden did not look as beautiful as it used to when Mehta Sir was around the mansion. The flowers looked faded and wilted. The chirping of the birds was also very faint and lifeless. Everything seemed to have stopped moving. Life had lost its charm and cheerfulness. It had come to a sudden halt bringing our lives to a standstill. I was going through shock followed by depression. But life does not give you time to grieve.

Aditya returned to the Mansion in June that year and turned the servants out as he wanted a new breed of servants to take over. He gave us twenty four hours to vacate the dorm. The servants were all shocked at his decision and the dormitory was in a state of pain and anguish and panic. We did not know where to go. We had not been given adequate time to look for an alternate occupation. Each one of us was frantically searching for some job or the other. Mani, Naval and I spoke about the next step in life. Lakhan came in the morning and learnt about Aditya's harsh decision. He sighed and sat down with us. All of us were quiet as our minds were running at the pace of a cheetah trying to decide how to find a new job soon. Lakhan looked at the sky and said," Sometimes it is easier to find the right direction in the changing winds". I soon found out the truth that lay hidden in Lakhan's statement. He had made a very meaningful statement that day. Lakhan informed us that he would try to find a job at the adjacent farm house. "It is not difficult to find a job but it is difficult to get a generous employer like Mehta Sir," Lakhan said in a hoarse voice. We all agreed as he was so right, we would never be able to find such a good employer like Mehta Sir. We were being treated like family at the Mehta Mansion. We had a place to stay and got good meals and such perks were not easy to get from other employers. His attitude towards us had also been very good which would not be easy to match for any other employer. Mrs. Mehta had also been very generous and kind to us. We could not find such employers ever in our life. We had been fortunate to be working at Mehta Mansion but our stay here had been limited by time. Mani, Naval and I were on the streets struggling to face reality. It was like the time when I had first moved to Gaulpur but now my savings were higher and I had the experience to face hardships offered by the city and of course I had built some contacts that I could look up to in the time of need.

I met Mrs. Mehta before I left the Mansion. She was as gentle as ever and felt sorry that I had to leave the Mansion. She asked me if I needed any money. "No Ma'am. I am ok. I have almost found a new job so I will be fine. Thanks so much for asking me Ma'am. I will take your leave now. It was a great opportunity to work for Sir and you and I was fortunate to get a job here," I thanked her as my eyes searched the house for a glimpse of Anita. "Suraj, you can come to me whenever you need any help. I will not ask you to stay as Aditya will not be nice to you and I know you will do better when you are away. But you can come back for any help," Mrs. Mehta said to me as I was leaving. I nodded and thanked her. It was a touching moment that ended with a smile when I caught a glimpse of Anita in the hallway. I wanted to say bye to her but could not. It was difficult and I was not sure whether I would see her again or not as I was unsure about what future had in store for me. I walked out of the main gate and turned around to take a last look at the Mansion when I saw Anita walking towards me. She came up to me and stood there for some time. "Bye Suraj, wish you all the best in life," she said to me. I could tell she wanted to say something to me but hesitated and stood there for some time. I waited for her to talk but she just said bye to me and her lips moved to give way to a faint smile. She asked me where I would be going and I did not have an answer to her question. I told her I will let her know soon when I find a place. I was hoping to speak to her at length but just could not say anything apart from goodbye. She was very quiet and looked upset at the situation. I was still unsure of her feelings for me but hoped to ask her and get a positive response from her soon. "Thanks Anita." I replied with a heavy heart as I did not want to say goodbye to her but I did and left from Mehta Mansion. I kept thinking about her while I walked back to Naval and Mani. It was impossible to leave the Mansion, or was it impossible to leave Anita there. I was feeling very low and the world seemed to close in on me. I was leaving a part of me with Anita. My heart tore and wrenched and my head asked me to move ahead in life. I felt so torn apart that it took time for me to collect all my pieces and put them together to move ahead in life.

It was a battle of the heart and the mind. I had still not given her the green silk sari that Ma had sent for her. It was lying in my grey bag waiting for the right moment. I had to move ahead and find the road to my destination in life. I knew for sure that I would return soon to give her the sari. I tried to pacify myself by believing that life was leading me in the direction that God wanted me to take and I should move with the flow. I had to believe in God's will and keep moving ahead in life till the final goal was attained. It was tough to leave Anita but I was not left with any other option. I knew that I would be coming back for her very soon and that kept me moving ahead. Those days were filled with hardships as it was not just the physical discomfort but the unbearable pain from the emotional torment that I was going through. I had to take all the hardships in my stride and move out of the Mehta Mansion. Life had changed a lot since the day I had landed at Gaulpur. My dreams had an inclusion now, and it was Anita. She had become an integral part of my life and my dreams of my future were built around her. I asked God to make the prophecy of the priest at Dori come true soon while I walked out of the Mansion.

Mani, Naval and I had been contemplating on the next step in life. Mani wanted to go back to his home town Alsi to be with his family. He planned to settle down in Alsi in case he found any job there. He was happy to return to Alsi as this would give him more time with his wife and children and his parents. He was hopeful of getting a job at one of the factories in Alsi. "There is no dearth of jobs anywhere, as long as one is willing to work," Mani said hopefully. "Yes, I do agree and feel that you will be able to get a job soon at Alsi," I replied with a sigh. I did not want to see him go. It felt like a family

111

slowly tearing apart as everyone left one by one. Naval and I went with him to the railway station to bid him goodbye. Naval had found a job at one of the restaurants close by. Naval had worked at this restaurant before joining Mehta Mansion and knew the manager so he was able to return to his old employer. The job did not pay him well but it was better than being unemployed. I had spoken to a small time contractor who was making a set of eight apartments near Rose Petals School. He needed a guard for his godown for a couple of months. He hired me at once as he was in an urgent need of a guard. He had torn down an old villa and was building apartments on the plot. Mani, Naval and I were taking separate paths towards our new lives. It was yet another goodbye. I was at the contractor's office the next morning. The apartments near Rose Petals School were called Rose View Apartments. I waited for three hours for the contractor to come to the site. The contractor Sajan was a six feet tall hefty and very pushy, arrogant and mean man who started his day screaming at the top of his voice. He used foul and abusive language whenever he spoke to anyone and his comments were sharp and nasty making him very unpopular with his staff. I learnt in due course that he believed that his staff worked only when he shouted at them. I had to manage the godown that had the stock for the construction site. The godown was a temporary room built near the construction site to store the construction material. I had to be on duty at night and I slept in the godown during the day when the second guard was on duty. I had lined some sacks of cement horizontally to make a bed for myself. I was again without a bed but this time my make shift home was a little more comfortable than the railway platform as it had walls around it and there was no noise from the trains or passengers or vendors. My body was divided into portions as I lay on the row of sacks with gaps in between though I tried to cover the gaps with empty sacks that I folded and stuffed in the crevices. It was cool inside the godown so I was lucky to be away from the scorching heat outside. It was almost an year since I had landed in Gaulpur and life had seen multiple ups and downs since then. I was going with the flow of life and letting it lead me to where life intended to go. But this is not what I had set out for and this led to rising unrest within me. I had come to a point when I was frustrated beyond all limits and my temper would easily shoot up at the slightest instigation. I would pick up fights with the other guard on duty and I was unhappy with the unpleasant situation I was in. I had to do a lot of self talking to bring back normalcy in my life and in my behavior as I knew that losing my temper would not lead me anywhere. This was not a solution for improving my situation or for moving ahead in life. I tried to think like a matured person and got control of myself. I kept calling out to God for help but help did not seem to be coming soon. I was like a free bird that had been caged by my situation and I wanted to break free immediately. I would peck at the wires of my cage and fall back in despair.

*C*hapter 22

Being a guard is not easy. I was awake while the world slept in peace. The other guard relieved me at eight in the morning. I walked around the godown like doing a *parikrama* at the temple. The sky was quiet and so was the world around me. There was very little activity on the road after ten in the night. I could only see trucks pass by on the road after ten. The shadows of the dark night would get illuminated by the high beams of the trucks that flew by at night and the light would fade away as the vehicles moved ahead. I would count the number of times a light beam pierced through the pitch darkness of the road and the number of times it missed falling on the pole in front of the godown. My duty as a guard was tough and overall a very boring task. I would chant the *Gayatri Mantra* at times and sing some songs while I waited to greet dawn. Some trucks passed by at night with such speed that I would get swept off my feet with the strong current of air they generated with their velocity. I had to hold to the ground firmly when the trucks flew by. I spent the night guarding the godown and taking stock of the items there. It was a job that came with a big responsibility as the stock was worth millions. Sajan had given me a gun but I was hoping that I would not need to use it.

It was the third night of my duty when I heard some sparking. I searched for the source of the noise and saw sparks coming out from the wires of a pole adjacent to the godown. There was a short circuit at the pole which had created these fireworks. A small fire broke out soon and the flames moved towards the godown. The flames were growing in size and moving with high speed towards the godown. I ran to the sand bags inside the godown to pull out a bag. It took some minutes before I could reach the sand bags as there were some wooden planks in the way. The fire was growing stronger and so was my worry. I dragged the sand bag out of the godown, ripped it open and used the sand to diffuse the fire. One bag was not sufficient so I got another bag and then another. It took five bags to fully control the fire. I was totally exhausted by the end of the fifth trip. I made sure that the fire had been diffused and then called Sajan from the landline at the godown to inform him about the fire. Sajan returned to examine the godown. There was ample proof for him to see and believe that I was telling the truth. I knew he was a man who would easily get suspicious and blame me for having caused the fire. He inspected the place and realized that I did not have anything to do with the breakout of the fire. I showed him the pole and the burnt wooden plank near the godown. There was sand all over the burnt plank and he was able to visualize the event that had taken place at the godown. He thanked me for saving the godown and went home. My duty got over after three hours and I got a chance to relax. I fell on my sack bed with a loud thud and slept well. Life was moving at a snail's pace and my job was the most boring job in the world. I would walk around the godown at night and plan about my new job. It took ages for the night to get over. Each minute seemed like an year. I felt the clock was forgetting to work at night. The seconds hand seemed to stand still and the minutes hand also froze making the night seem endless. I spent the time drawing imaginary figures in the dark shadows of the night. I was trudging lazily around the godown like a turtle with its head hanging out of the shell. It was not just the endless night but the fact that this job was short lived which made me restless. I had to find another job soon as this job was temporary. I tried to wake up in the afternoon and go on my job hunt. I was on the verge of letting frustration overcome me as I felt I was confined and wanted to break free of all my bonds and fly towards my dreams. It was a very restricting situation and I wanted it to be over soon. The thought of going around in circles and watching the godown itself was frustrating. I was on the lookout for a new job and could not wait for this job to get over.

It was at this site that I met Babu. Babu would bring tea for Sajan's staff. Babu was a four and a half feet tall young man whose enthusiasm was in deep contrast to his dwarfish height. He carried a big smile on his face throughout the day. I had always seen him in a red T shirt with grey pajamas and blue flip flops. He hopped around the site with a kettle and disposable cups and a bag of *mathris*. He would pour out tea in the cups and hand them over to Sajan's staff. Sajan was given complimentary tea and *mathris* by Babu as an incentive for letting him enter his construction site. He charged five rupees for a cup of tea. Some people also bought *mathris* from him. *Mathri* was priced the same as a tea cup. His kettle and *mathri* bag would get empty within minutes and he had to make a second trip to cover the entire staff at the site. He had a man assisting him and they took turns in making tea and serving it. His stock vanished in no time as we gobbled up all that he got even before he could return with a refill. His business looked like a profitable one as the demand for tea can never deplete and this attracted my attention. The demand for tea had to grow with the growth in population and this tea business was not even seasonal so there was scope for running it throughout the year. In fact the demand for tea would increase manifold during winters. Everything about this business was very positive. I was weighing the pros and cons and could see a good number of pros for taking up this business. I was thinking of speaking to Naval and Raja before taking the final decision about this new business that I was planning to jump into. I also wanted Ma and Papa's opinion on my decision so I called them up from a phone booth. They were excited to hear my voice. Ma was more receptive to my idea and Papa was just as apprehensive as expected. They both had their share of advice for me. Ma wanted me to take the leap as she knew I had big dreams and she was confident that I could manage it. She also knew that I had to take a leap someday else I would never be able to achieve what I had set out for. Papa started to think and gave me his unbiased opinion about the business with a long list of all the associated risks. His advice was just short of a big 'No' for the business. He was not at ease with the idea. He wanted me to take the easiest possible path of being employed with someone and not get into the headache of managing a business. He found the idea of being an employer very risky and bothersome and of course he did not want to see his son under any stress or tension. I spoke to them for forty minutes and tried to convince them that I would take my decision keeping into account all the risks and take all the necessary precautions so that there is least bit of stress to manage. Ma blessed me and wished me good luck. Papa kept saying, "Think well before you take any decision about this business idea of yours. I am with you in whatever decision you take." I had made up my mind. I knew that this was the beginning of the road to my dream and I had to take this leap. It was now or never. I later called Raja and asked him if he wanted to join me in my new business. He did not sound very keen about the idea. "This job at the NextEdge BPO is ok for me. I am not suited for a tough job and running a business is definitely tough. Here I am spending the day stamping documents and making entries in a register. The day is not very tiring as my work is concentrated to a few hours of the day. I just laze for the rest of the time. A tea stall is surely not my cup of tea!!" he told me frankly in a jovial tone about his inability to join my business. I knew he was easy go lucky and was even surprised to find him working at the BPO so his decision did not come as a shock to me. Nevertheless I wanted to ask him for the sake of our friendship. Now I had to check with Naval and I was hopeful that he would agree to join my new business. I went to meet Babu before I set out to the restaurant where Naval worked.

Babu had a small kiosk for his tea stall near the site. The tea stall seemed to flourish as I always saw it flooded with customers. It was difficult to see Babu as he was forever hidden behind the customers who surrounded his stall. He told me how he set up his tea stalls near new construction sites and offices. He was sending all his savings to his wife at his village where he had managed to build a house with the money that he was saving from the stall. I was inspired by his story and started to dream about owning a tea stall of my own. First it was Sundar who had impressed me at the railway platform with his tea stall business and now Babu was motivating me to enter this line of business. Tea, the elixir of life was beckoning me to get into this flourishing trade. It was then that I knew why I enjoyed watching tea in the making and how its colour made me feel overjoyed and its aroma had me mystified. There was a karmic connection between tea and me and this was now going to form into a bond with a strong flavour! I was dreaming about my stall and I was pouring tea into cups for customers and collecting big cash for it. I was already hearing the clatter of kettle and tea cups. My dreams were brewing tea in the pan of my life! I seemed to be sailing through a stream of tea in a cup shaped boat made with tea leaves and tea bags and spoon shaped oars to paddle it. Sugar grains seemed like small islands on the way. I was floating in a pool of tea with a *mathri* as my float. I was totally engulfed in the thoughts of my new business which was going to take off soon. It was a very comforting feeling, a feeling of achievement, a feeling that I was close to seeing my dreams shape up soon.

I had planned to start a tea stall in downtown Gaulpur near the BPOs. I could run this twenty four by seven as the BPOs run round the clock. I did not need an elaborate infrastructure to run the stall. I could manage with a canvas tarpaulin and one bench and a stove, cooking gas cylinder, utensils for making and serving tea, ingredients for making tea and disposable cups. I could later add biscuits, *mathris*, chips, snacks and chocolates once my business would take off. I could also hire someone to assist me in my business once it was stabilized. I was planning my business from start to finish with all the possible details that I could think of. I still had my grey bag with me but it was bloated by now with the addition of my regular clothes and woollens and of course the sari that Ma had given me for Anita. I only had the grey bag as my possession and was going to start a business with my savings. I was optimistic and ready to take off into the skies. This was going to be my first flight and I had no help from anyone at that juncture. I was nervous and excited at the same time. It was going to be a big and important move in my life and I knew it would change things for the better. God was designing my life as per my desires for me. I asked Sajan to lend me an old worn out canvas tarpaulin from his site and set out on my mission to start the tea stall. Sajan had a number of tarpaulins that he was using at his construction sites and gave me an old worn out one from the godown. "You can take this one and need not return it," he said. It was probably his way of thanking me for saving his godown from the fire the other night. I thanked Sajan and went to meet Naval to inform him about my upcoming business with a lot of enthusiasm. Naval was busy serving some customers so I waited for him to get free. Naval looked frail and he seemed to have aged within days. It must be tough and stressful at the restaurant for him I thought. Naval got free after twenty minutes. He waved at me to meet him outside the restaurant. I walked out to a shop next to the restaurant and waited for Naval to join me. Naval came ten minutes later and I told him about the new business idea. Naval seemed excited to know about it and expressed his desire to join the business. "What about your job at the restaurant?" I asked him. "It is not what I had expected it to be. I rarely get to cook. I am serving food most of the times and am surviving on tips from customers. This is not what I had wanted from this job. I would prefer to be with you in partnership. We can do wonders together," he said. I was happy to have him with me. "Let us go and meet Babu, you too will get inspired when you meet him," I said. "And we can even get some good tips from him for running our new business." Naval and I went to meet Babu. We were there to talk to him in detail on how to run our new business. We were impressed at how Babu was running his business. Babu was over obliging and he even offered to help us set up the stall. He started by telling us all that would be required to set up the stall. I had thankfully bought the major items so I knew that I was on the right track. We went to the site which I had selected and set up our tea stall there. I was carrying with me the bag that had all the new kitchen items I had purchased for the stall. The site was just amazing and perfect for the tea stall. It was a corner tree on the road near a BPO. It was strategically located as anyone getting in or out of the BPO gate would notice the stall. The tree was dense and could provide a good shade from the sun. The corner had a good space where people could even park their cars or scooters and walk up to our stall for tea. This could also help in getting business from people passing by on vehicles. There were some more BPOs in the vicinity so we were expecting a reasonable footfall at our stall. I looked at the spot with immense admiration in my eyes. I was feeling proud to have selected an apt spot for my tea stall. I kept staring at the tree as this was going to mark the beginning of a new phase in my life. I had waited and struggled a lot to get to this phase of my life and I just could not help keep my happiness to myself. My smile and my joy were becoming infectious as everything around me seemed to be happy. The branches of the tree were swaying slowly as though they were dancing to soft music. The breeze was blowing into a soft song and caressing my cheeks gently in an effort to let me know that good times had begun. I named the tree my 'Chai-Tree'. I looked at Naval and Babu and they too were very happy with the location that I had selected for our tea stall. Life was leading me to my goal and I was at peace with myself and also excited to know that life was unfolding a new chapter for me. It was a moment of great happiness and pride for me and I wished that Ma, Papa, Anita and Raja could be with me to cherish that moment with me. I was missing them immensely so I let out a sigh. Babu turned to me with a quizzical look on his face. I nodded that things were fine. I then moved my attention to the purpose for which we had come to the spot. We were there to set our tea stall and lay the foundation stone for the beginning of a new phase of our life. I turned to Babu and Naval and we spoke about how we should set the canvas tarpaulin so that the kitchen is arranged under the shade of the tarpaulin and we leave enough room for us to move around to serve our customers. Babu quickly set the blue and white striped tarpaulin for us. He was very swift and light on his feet. He climbed the tree and tied the tarpaulin to its branches and trunk with the expertise of a trapeze artist. He spread some sacks on the ground for covering its undulating contours and helped us with the layout of our kitchen and pantry area under the tree. I went back to Sajan for some old planks of wood that would serve as our kitchen counter. We managed to get some bricks from a construction site nearby to use as leg support for our kitchen counter. Babu had our kitchen counter ready in a jiffy. Then he chopped a part of one of the wooden planks into a tile that was two feet long and one foot wide. "What is this tile for?" I asked Babu.

"You need to write the name of your stall on this tile. We will hang it on one of the branches of this tree," Babu told me in his hoarse grunting voice. He found a piece of coal for me to write on the tile. I wrote '*Apki Chai*' on the tile and handed it to Babu. He made two holes in the tile and strung a rope through it and hung it on a branch of the tree. I walked towards the other side of the road to see if the tile was visible from a distance. I found the tile to be prominently placed and thanked Babu for all his help. I chanted the *Gayatri Mantra* with a request to God to help us in succeeding in our mission. This is how my first business got inaugurated. We were up and running in no time.

The kitchen looked very inviting as it had everything displayed very neatly. We put the pan on the stove and made the first pale of tea. One of the security guards from the nearby building was our first customer for the day. We could not hold back our smiles and excitement when we saw him walk towards our stall. We both stared at him while he moved towards us. Our eyes were glued to him as he walked from the other end of the road to us. We were first unsure whether he was walking towards us or not. We looked around and did not see anything else which could have attracted his attention and that gave us the confidence that he was walking to our stall. We were anxious, curious, excited and tense as our eyes moved with him from across the road till he reached our stall and we did not blink even once for the fear of losing sight of him. We felt relieved to see him come up to us and stop. He looked around the stall while we had our gaze fixed on him. We looked at him with great expectations. We could not wait for him to give us his order. "A new tea stall, hmm, looks good" he said in a husky voice. "How much is a cup of tea? And how much is the *mathri*?" he inquired while his fingers played a drum on our table. "Five rupees each," both Naval and I said in chorus. His eyebrows played a hop and skip and he let out a squeal from his husky throat, "Ok, give me a cup of tea." We quickly poured him a cup of tea. We gave him a complimentary *mathri* with his tea as he had set our clock in motion. He handed us five rupees and thanked us for the free *mathri* before he left. That five rupee note was the first sale of our first day of business. This note was priceless and we planned to keep it in our small temple that we intended to have at our stall. We took turns to hold the note with great pride as it was our first earning from the business. This security guard became our permanent customer who came to us for tea and *mathri* three times in a day. He was our first and a very special customer. I kept praying to God to be with us and see us through the day with success. I called Ma and Papa in the evening to give them the good news. They were very happy for me. It was the first time that I heard something positive from Papa. He seemed to have gained some confidence in me and that motivated me to a great extent. I invited Raja to our stall the very next morning. He dropped by on way to NextEdge. He was thrilled on seeing our tea stall. "This is superb! Great job guys! This is really very impressive. I was not expecting such a good layout. You have chosen a great spot too. This spot is the best and will help in getting a lot of customers. I would love to be here but do not like to work so . . . you know . . . . I will just visit you guys off and on. But I am very happy to see you all and your stall," Raja said in an excited tone. Raja was very happy for us and that made me happier. My dreams were going to get a direction now. That was our first day at business. Our ship had finally set sail. The direction of the wind was favourable and waters were also calm making our ship sail smoothly. We got about ten customers on the first day. The numbers went to twenty five on the second day and then there was no looking back as we did not need to count the people who would come to us for tea. We had repeat customers who would come to us after every hour or two hours. We were brewing pales and pales of tea during the day. Our stall was humming with the conversation of office goers with intermittent slurps from them with the clatter of utensils in the background. Our stall was filled with the aroma and sizzling steam of tea leaves. Customers were flocking our stall just like they did at Babu's tea stall. It was an overwhelming moment to see our business picking up just as we had intended it to. We were running around the stall serving tea to our customers. We did not get a moment's break as our stall was busy throughout the day. Customers kept coming till late in the evening. We closed by eleven at night and resumed our service at six in the morning. It was twelve thirty by the time we wrapped up and went to sleep. We had to wake up at four in the morning to have the stall operating by six. We were getting a few hours of sleep but our enthusiasm kept us moving and did not let us feel tired in spite of all the hard work that we put in during the day. Life was challenging and exciting at the same time. We were willing to put in all the effort that we could as long as good results flowed in.

Chapter 23

I remembered Lakhan's golden words," Sometimes it is easier to find the right direction in the changing winds". I realized that Lakhan was a very wise man. His words spoke of his great wisdom. I was living the truth of his statement. I had to thank Aditya for turning me out of the Mehta Mansion. He had made me realize my dreams by throwing me out of the Mansion else I would not have thought about starting my own business. I could now feel that his decision was God sent as it had changed the course of my life catapulting me directly towards my dreams. Aditya seemed like God's magic wand to me at that point of time. He had helped me by moving me closer to my dreams. The winds of change had taken their decision for me and I was flowing with them to my goals in life. I was getting positive signals from life as it seemed to be moving in the right direction now.

Two months later we were rejoicing at our decision of opening the tea stall as we were in high profits and our savings were building up. Most of our customers chatted with us as they waited for their tea and we got to hear about their office life. It was a different life altogether that they would create for us. I liked to hear their stories and anecdotes from their office life. Our stall had turned into a pseudo marriage bureau as many couples sneaked out of office to discuss marriage proposals at our stall. We were turning into an entertainment hub where office politics ruled the box office chart predominantly. Their anecdotes were as spicy as any television show. Some customers had their family woes to discuss with others and these were also like the family soaps that are aired on television. We learnt a lot about the life history of our customers. We also learnt that office and home are both filled with politics where each person tries to outshine the others. Our customers spoke freely about their problems without realizing that we were around and could hear all that was being said. I was reminded of the Mehtas who hardly cared for my presence when they disclosed information about themselves while riding in the car. Our customers at the stall also ignored our presence and completely opened their heart out while they spoke about their problems and discussed their issues amongst themselves. Some customers found the stall to be an escape route from their workload as they came and relaxed at the stall for a long time before returning to their office. We benefitted from the customers who stayed longer at the stall as they added to our business revenue while they kept ordering for more tea. We were kept thoroughly engaged and entertained by our customers. We did not need to get a television or go to watch a movie at the multiplex as we were getting adequate entertainment at our business location itself. It was work and fun at the same time for us. Our business was two months old and we were running in profits. I was pouring tea for a customer when I heard a familiar voice, "I would like a nice hot cup of tea too". I looked up and was overwhelmed to see Mani standing in front of me. I just put the pan down on the table and stood there staring at Mani. I was not sure whether he was there for real or if I had again got into my day dreaming mode. Naval turned around and exclaimed, "Hey Mani, when did you return from Alsi?" Mani said, "Last night. I returned last night. Then I inquired about both of you and learnt you are here so I rushed to meet you." The two of us ran to Mani and lifted him and gave him a bump before dropping him on the floor. He lifted up like a hot air balloon and came down like 'humpty dumpty having a great fall'. "You are too heavy man, you are like a bag of bricks," shouted Naval as he tried to regain his breath. I was sitting on the ground panting. "Yes Mani, you are surely too heavy to lift, it seems you are carrying two extra people with you," I teased Mani. The three of us burst out laughing and hugged each other and joked around while our customers gaped at us in surprise. The three of us were sprawled on the ground and were laughing our heads off. I poured tea for the customers and then for us and we again sat down cross legged on the ground. "You will have to pay for this tea Mani," Naval said teasingly to Mani. Mani was choking and gasping for breath as he laughed. His paunch was like a football dribbling as he laughed like a maniac. Naval's moustache seemed to be dancing on his lip as he smiled. I was rolling on the floor as I could not stop laughing. My teeth seemed to fall out of my mouth as I laughed out loud. It was a beautiful moment that witnessed a reunion of friends and we were celebrating it with tea. It was great to have Mani back with us. We had been missing him and his jokes. We now had another person to share our worries with. We spoke at length at night and did not get to know when sleep took over and we were lost in our dreams. We now had a third partner with us and our joy had no limit. Business had to get better undoubtedly. Life at Alsi was not satisfying for

Mani and the job at the small oil factory did not pay him much so Mani had decided to return to Gaulpur. His wife was not happy with his decision but he had convinced her with a promise that he would call her to Gaulpur very soon. He had given all his savings to his wife and returned penniless to Gaulpur to make a new beginning once again. He was happy to have found us and happier to know we were in business, a business which he could join. He missed his children and wife but soon came to terms with reality as he was here only for their welfare. It felt great to be together again. We were together and bonding like a family again. This is the greatness of Gaulpur, it gives shelter to all who come to live here and it is able to get them a job sooner or later. It is a haven for people seeking employment. And the three of us were no exceptions to this rule of Gaulpur. Gaulpur had adopted us and we had adapted to its culture. There is something about Gaulpur that makes people stay here permanently. Anyone who comes here finds it difficult to leave this city. People get so entwined in Gaulpur's culture and lifestyle that they find it difficult to settle anywhere else. Gaulpur changes you, your life and your perspective at looking at everything in life. One matures very fast here as Gaulpur finds a way to teach you the lessons of the entire life in a limited period of time.

The three of us would crouch under the canvas tarpaulin at night to sleep. We had a joint purpose in life now. We wanted to build our business and make good profits. We did not want to hire a place to live as yet as we wanted to save as much as we could so the tarpaulin was our home for the time being. We were a small family living and working together. We were so tired by the end of the day that we just lay down and slept like babies crouched together under our tarpaulin. We would get up early morning and clean up the stall and set up the stove before the customers started to walk in. We divided the work amongst us every morning. One of us had an additional task to be on the lookout for customers straying to other stalls and coax them into coming to our stall somehow. Mani and I switched jobs to buy the groceries and other raw materials for the stall and clean the utensils. Naval was majorly involved in making tea. The three of us took turns to serve tea and collect cash. Naval added some ginger and herbs to the tea to give it a special taste that made customers wanting more and more of our tea. The aroma of the herbs filled the surroundings and attracted customers to our stall. Some customers had two cups in a row and some frequented our stall seven to eight times during the day. Some passersby and visitors to the BPOS also stopped at our stall to have tea. On the whole our business was running extremely well and we were in good profits. We were floating on the clouds of our success and taking pride in our decision and the fact that our hard work had yielded good results.

Chapter 24

Things were running smoothly for some weeks till the arrival of the monsoon that came down lashing with all its might and authority and caught us sadly unprepared. It was a thunderstorm that shook the whole city like a huge wave capsizing a giant ship. Gaulpur had almost got flooded within a few hours. I can still visualize the day that was washed in the rains to reveal our pettiness in comparison to the forces of nature. We seemed like small ants trying to save ourselves from giant animals and running to find a shelter. I can recollect the day vividly. It was early morning and I was dreaming about Anita. She looked a little tired but smiled at me as I walked up to her. She wanted to say something to me but stopped and looked around. It was an endless wait as I stood there wanting to hear her speak to me when I felt a drop of water on my cheek. I touched my cheek and woke up from my dream as I felt a drizzle on my face. Anita was nowhere to be seen. I looked around to find Anita and realized I was dreaming. Mani and Naval also woke up. We were in the midst of trying to comprehend the situation when it started to pour heavily. The rain came down in huge waves aiming to uproot our very being. The waves looked like monsters with enormous fangs and red devilish eyes that were springing down to devour us completely. The sound of the downpour was so loud that we could barely hear each other talk. Everything around us was soaked and we were wading through streams of water. The bag of tea leaves had opened with the force of the wind throwing the tea leaves on the road and they were soon floating in the pool of water and the milk pan had also overturned. We fortunately saved the sugar box from drowning. We quickly gathered the rest of our belongings from the stall and took shelter under a tree. We literally paddled with our feet through the heavy stream of water. We looked at our tea stall being uprooted by the storm. I could very well relate our situation to the saying 'Man proposes and God disposes'. It was a continuous downpour coming like the wrath of the heavens from the skies above that did not seem to have any intention to stop or reduce its intensity. Our home and means of livelihood were washed away completely. We looked at the floating tea leaves that were flowing into the pool of milk that was moving towards the drain on the side of the road. "There goes our week's supply of tea leaves," said Mani in his depressed voice. Naval sighed heavily and I looked around to find a place where we could keep our belongings shielded from the rain. Water was drenching us and I was reminded of my first day in Gaulpur when I had walked out of the railway platform to soak myself in Gaulpur's rain. There was a marked difference between the two days. The first day in Gaulpur was a new day for me and that rain was like a welcome song for me. It had felt nice to be drenched by that rain as I had nothing to lose. This downpour was destructive and was like a warning signal telling us that we had to be well prepared for all seasons. The first rain was very gentle and calm but this rain could have claimed us with its grave intensity. We were huddled under the tree with our feet immersed in one foot deep water waiting for the rain to stop. It felt like standing in a swamp waiting for a boat to show up and rescue us. We were shipwrecked and rescue was nowhere in sight. It was amusing that I was cursing the rain for spoiling my dream and not for uprooting our stall. I was surprised and also amused with myself as Anita had indeed become the most important person in my life and she had grown to be my first priority as I could only think about her even in a dire situation like the one we were in. The crisis was not affecting me as it had intended to. I knew we would bounce back and set our shop with ease again. It was a long wait before the sun rose and lit up the sky. We put up our stall again. It took hours for our clothes to dry and days for the pool of water around our stall to dry up completely. We were not prepared for the monsoon. But now we did not want to leave anything to chance. We thought about giving our stall a good shade from the rain and the sun. It was important to do so even if it meant spending a heavy sum on infrastructure as we did not want to suffer again. Naval went to the local wholesale market to find a waterproof sheet that we could use to cover our stall during rains. It took him half a day to find a giant size waterproof sheet that could easily cover our stall. We felt much safer with the sheet in our possession. He got four poles to tie the sheet and another waterproof sheet to spread under the canvas tarpaulin like a sleeping bag for us. Naval and Mani held the sheet while I tied it to the four poles. My height came in handy again. The sheet provided good coverage for our stall and saved us from the sun and rain. The old canvas tarpaulin had got more than a dozen holes in it and was too worn out to shield us from heat and rain. We disposed off the old, torn and damaged tarpaulin and rejoiced in the comfort of the shade and shelter of our new waterproof sheet. Our cost for the day had gone up too high as we had to buy our tea supplies that had been spoilt by the rain but we managed to break even by late evening as we got a huge number of customers who wanted to have tea to fight the cold breeze that was blowing after the rain. It was a day of running around throughout that left us tired by the evening. The three of us slept like little puppies after the struggle filled day. The next morning was very sunny with business running at the usual pace keeping the three of us well occupied. We could not think beyond our tea and kettles. We were making and serving tea like clockwork. Our speed improved day by day and we were making tea at express speed within weeks. Life was back to normalcy soon. Our business was rocking and things were progressing as we had planned. We were busy throughout the day and that kept the money flowing in. The sun would wake us up with a desire for the money and the moon would put us to bed with the fulfillment of our desire. We were surrounded by customers and the aroma of tea throughout the day. It was a great experience to be running our own show. We were not dependent on anybody for orders or for taking a decision. We were our own masters and that made every day very special. We were totally inspired to look forward to each day with complete enthusiasm and high spirits. The kettles, cups, pans and tea were just not the means to our livelihood but they had become our companions whom we treasured with total pride and utmost care.

I was surprised to see Raja at our stall one afternoon. Raja usually visited us either on way to his office or on his way back. We did not usually see him in the afternoons.

Raja was going to Murli for a week and had come to meet us before leaving for his vacation. "I am going to Murli for a week Suraj. Do you want to send any message to Ma and Papa?" he asked. I nodded and asked him to wait while I ran to the nearby shopping complex to get some gifts for my parents that I could send home with Raja. I walked around some shops and found it difficult to decide what to get for my parents. I had little savings and too many desires as I wanted to buy them a number of things. I went from one shop to the other but could not get what I really wanted to due to my limited savings which curtailed my spending. I kept looking at the price tags of things to decide what to buy for my parents. Each time I looked at a price tag my hand withdrew itself as things were priced very high and my savings did not allow me to buy anything. I walked to another market near the BPO where the prices were lower than what I had just seen. At last I found some things which I could afford. I bought a cotton sari for Ma and a *dhoti kurta* for Papa. I gave Raja some money to handover to Ma. I also wrote a small note for my parents that Raja could take back with the gifts. I wanted to send more money but my savings were little. I hugged him as though I was hugging Ma and Papa. He was my link to my parents at that point of time. I still could not afford to buy a mobile phone and was dependent on the phone booth to speak to my parents. I hugged him again and bid him goodbye. I offered him a job again but he refused. He wanted an easy job and did not want to take on any stress. I was in a deep pensive mood when Raja left. I was missing my parents and I wanted to save more so that I could help my parents to a greater extent financially. This meant that I had to expand the business to generate more revenue.

I was thinking hard on how we could take our business some notches higher than where we were. I was also contemplating on looking at a different line of business but could not come up with something concrete. I was unsure of how we could expand this business. I was lucky to have friends like Mani and Naval who were totally dedicated to their work and had never complained about anything. We were all putting in our best in running our business but we had to think beyond this business to increase our earnings. I kept walking aimlessly in search of an answer that was hidden somewhere but was not visible as yet. I thought of meeting Babu to help find answers to my questions as it was Babu who had made me take the decision for starting this business initially. I was hopeful of getting a direction after meeting him. I went to meet Babu in the evening. Babu was busy making *pakoras* when I reached his stall. "Is that a new addition to your stall? Looks good and tempting," I commented looking at his stall's new look and new additions. "Yes, this is new and a great hit with the crowd. The aroma of the *pakoras* attracts customers and they end up buying tea and many other things from me". I looked around the stall and saw Babu had included cookies, chips, *pakoras*, chocolates and mints to his menu at the stall. It was an impressive layout that had me thinking about our stall. I looked around to see how Babu had organized his stall to see if we were missing anything in our layout. Babu's stall was properly organized and it resembled a fully operational household kitchen in action. He had placed all the raw material very close to the stove making his movement minimal as he had to serve a number of customers with least help and within a limited timeframe. I walked back to our stall realizing that this was God's indication to me to help me decide the next move for enhancing my business further. I only had to get Mani and Naval convinced with the idea to make this move happen. I thought it would be best for them to see this live in action to agree to the idea. I got Mani and Naval to meet Babu the next evening. I made two trips to Babu's stall, one with Naval and another trip with Mani as we did not want to leave our stall unattended. I did not tell them about the additions to Babu's stall as I wanted to surprise them. We reached Babu's stall and the first thing that caught our attention was the wok with *pakoras* frying in it. Babu was turning the *pakoras* around in the oil to ensure that they were well cooked from all sides. The crisp brown colour of the *pakoras* could tempt anyone and the aroma from the wok was rising and filling the surrounding air with temptation. It could attract anybody from a good distance. We were drooling at the sight of *pakoras*. I wanted to capture the expression on Mani and Naval's faces and I could see that Babu's addition to his business impressed Mani and Naval just in line with my expectations. Naval tasted both the chutneys that Babu was making with the *pakoras*. I could tell from the look on his face that he did not like any of the chutneys. Naval's cooking was far superior and he was known to make very delicious rare delicacies so how could he like these plain chutneys! "How is the chutney, you do not seem to be enjoying its taste," I asked Naval. "It is awful, it tastes like rotten potatoes topped with chillies," he said. Naval was very straight forward in his approach to life and his opinions were always honest. I nodded my head and planned not to taste the rotten potato chutney. We ordered a plate of *pakoras* in each trip and polished them off in no time. Mani went around the stall looking at the stock of things Babu had added to his stall. Mani could not help picking up a *pakora* as we spoke to Babu. He quickly ate the *pakora* and reached for another one. I nudged him to stop. Mani made a face at me as he really wanted to eat to his heart's desire but I did not let him do so. Babu was a great cook. He had now employed two helpers for cooking and serving. The stall had a very good number of customers waiting to be served. It was an inspiring facade and we were getting motivated to make similar changes to our stall too. Mani and Naval were soon speaking the same language as mine and we were going to change our tea stall into a snack shop. It was good to hear them talking about it with full excitement as that made taking the decision extremely simple. They had been greatly inspired by what they saw at Babu's stall. It was easy to convince them by showing them the stall live in action. Babu had a special knack for business which reflected in whatever he did. He had figured out what would sell the most and had explored the opportunity very well. We could not stop talking about the *pakoras* and the effect they had on Babu's business. We discussed the list of things that we needed to set up our snack shop and also how to manage our funds for it. We were soon ready with our master plan and blueprint of our shop with all the raw materials and their layout so that we could cook and serve without too much running around between the pantry and cooking stove. Everything was written clearly in our memory as that is how we functioned. We would rehearse every detail in our memory before we hit the bed at night. There was a lot of work to be done before we could set up our little snack outlet. We had to make multiple arrangements and get our stall well equipped before setting forth with our business expansion plan. We planned on each item and where we would buy it from.

Mani and Naval knew Gaulpur more than I did and were aware of the wholesale markets where things could be bought at reasonable rates.

Our plan materialized in less than a month when we had made arrangements for all the raw materials and utensils required for our upcoming snack shop. It took us time to collect all that we needed for our shop. We had to carefully select the cookware as we wanted the price to be affordable and quality just reasonable. We compared the price of disposable crockery with steel and chinaware and decided to get steel utensils as they were the most cost effective. Our snack shop was up and running soon. Our menu included *pakoras* and *samosas* to start with. Naval made the most amazing chutney that I had ever had in my life. The chutney was created with minced mint, basil, coriander, onion and spinach that he would add to a bowl of curd and blend everything together really well and had our customers guessing about its ingredients. The ratio of these ingredients was only known to Naval as he had patented the recipe. The coriander and mint leaves gave the chutney a very unique flavour with a heavenly aroma that customers were unable to resist. Naval created magic with the *pakoras* as they were crispy yet they would melt in the mouth leaving one wanting more and more. The triangular *samosas* were amazingly delicious. They were filled to the ends with mashed potatoes and had a golden brown crust that had a fine crispness and texture. Customers came especially for the chutney that was growing famous day by day. We had to get a bigger stall and a better place to run our business from. The three of us took turns in exploring the city for a new place to set up our business. The shops were expensive and rents beyond our means. We were still not in a position to afford the rent of a shop so we started to look for a cheaper alternative that we could manage with ease. Each one of us took an hour off every day to explore the nearby localities to find a suitable place for our new snack shop. We even checked with Babu and Raja if they had seen any good spot in the city or the outskirts where we could start our new business.

*C*hapter 25

Mani found a nice spot for our new place of business and it was not going to cost us anything. I came up with a suggestion for the shop. The three of us visited the spot and inspected it like a community of builders coming up with a big shopping mall. We looked at every detail of the site and its surroundings. We counted the number of buildings around the spot and looked for other stalls in the vicinity. There was only one stall diagonally across the road at a distance from this spot. These buildings were new and there was only one stall to feed them. Our experiences and training from Mehta Mansion were coming in handy here. We were behaving like Mehta Sir and trying to think like accomplished businessmen. We were soon convinced that this was the best spot for our shop. There was a good need for a tea and snack stall in the area and we were all willing to provide it immediately. It was the right time to move to this spot before other stalls came up and grabbed our business opportunity. The three of us discussed it at length over a cup of tea and *samosas* and took the big decision!! We were soon going to set up our shop at the spot identified by Mani. We had to work on the kiosk that would work as our shop. We came up with a great idea for our kiosk. Naval and I met Khan Sahib, owner of the workshop where we used to get

Mehta Sir's cars repaired. We narrated our entire tale to him and appraised him of our requirement. He instantly agreed to help us. Khan Sahib called a friend of his who took us to a junkyard close by and helped us choose a car. We picked up an old van which was totally rusted and did not have any wheels. Khan Sahib was kind enough to send it to our new business spot next morning. The three of us took turns to paint the van. We scrubbed off the old paint and rust throughout the day. It took a whole day to get the old paint off the van. We kept scrubbing it till its entire surface was smooth. We devoted the next day to painting it. Our brush strokes stroked our new baby with love and passion as we painted it. Our love for our van and our passion for our business showed in the smoothness of the van's body that was now being covered with a white sheet of paint. Our van looked like a white pigeon that had flown out of its nest for the first time. We were proud parents of a new born baby and could not stop admiring our van. It needed four coats of paint to make it look presentable. "You have turned it into a white pigeon," a passerby commented. We smiled at him and nodded in agreement. Mani giggled and said, "Hope it does not fly away with our snacks." Mani again giggled and remarked, "Let us call our stall White Pigeon or may be let us name it *Safed Kabootar*." Naval grinned while I shook my head. It was a unanimous decision to call our new shop '*Chutney Haat*'. We painted the name of our shop on one side of our van in red colour that was clearly visible from a distance. Our shop was finally ready and so were we. *Chutney Haat* was the old white van from the junkyard that we had painted ourselves and given it the look of a small kiosk. Our kiosk was parked under a large tree on four piles of bricks that assumed the role of its wheels. We were in the city's commercial hub called Golden Plaza. Our kiosk was in a corner of one of the by lanes near a parking lot. This business could work wonders as we had a strategic spot and office goers always look for cheap stalls for snacks and lunch. Though we were not very close to the offices but the aroma of our *pakoras* could attract anyone from a distance. There were three smooth rocks on the roadside which we pushed to our stall to use as stools for our customers to sit. We put up a blue umbrella over the three rocks to give the stools some shade from the sun. We were becoming very innovative as our business progressed. We had removed the driver and passenger seats and moved them to one side of the van. The other side was our work space. One of the windows was used as a cash collection counter and the other for handing out snacks to customers. Cooking was done behind the van and our pantry was inside the van below the snack delivery window. We had a small blackboard hung outside the van where the menu was scribbled with a white chalk. I was the menu writer as I had the best handwriting out of the three of us. Every night we would load our van with all our belongings that were spread around the van and cover the van with the waterproof sheet. The van seats became our beds at night. Our beds were more comfortable now and we had a roof on our heads. Our sheet covered our van in the shape of an igloo making us feel like Eskimos in the comfort of our van home. We were all set for our business.

Naval was the main chef and Mani and I were his obedient assistants. Our Trio of Suraj, Mani and Naval was working together like an assembly line. Mani was chopping the vegetables, Naval mixed them in the gram flour and spices and rolled them into balls and I fried them. A plate of *pakoras* had eight dumplings in it, two each of potatoes, onions, cauliflower and spinach and of course our famous chutney was the accompaniment to the *pakoras*. We gradually introduced bread *pakoras* and *paneer pakoras* and *kachoris* to our menu. Naval showed us how to fry the *pakoras* so that they remain soft yet crisp and juicy. He had a trick on how to set the temperature at the right degree for the *pakoras* to get that golden brown colour and how and when to turn the *pakoras* in the oil. His culinary skills were a great asset to our business. He gave us lessons on how to chop the vegetables to the finest possible width. He was not happy the way Mani and I were chopping vegetables. "Cut them into thin slices and each slice should have the same width and length. Do you know it is the art of chopping that determines the taste of *pakoras*?" Naval said in his hoarse voice as he chopped the onion into the thinnest possible slices that were as transparent as the air around us. Mani picked up a slice of onion and it slipped from his fingers as it was too thin to hold. "Are you sure we need to have them so thin Naval, are these not too thin for *pakoras*?" Mani asked Naval inquisitively. Naval shook his head and gave us his Professor kind of look, the look that a teacher has when he looks through a pair of glasses that have slipped to the lower half of his nose. "No, they are just right. I like them just this size and they will make the best *pakoras* in the world," Naval told us convincingly with his big eyes peeping at us through his imaginary pair of glasses. We nodded and obeyed his instructions and tried to match his perfection. He was a perfectionist when it came to cooking. His passion and perfection showed in the way he chopped the vegetables and went through every detail and quality of ingredients. We could never match his passion but helped him in every possible way that we could. His flair for cooking was unbeatable in every respect. I was in charge of the stock and had to keep a check on every ingredient and raw material so that we were adequately stocked and did not have to make any last minute purchases. We would take turns to serve the snacks and collect cash. Cash started to pour in and we divided it into four parts, one part each for the three of us and the fourth portion for running the shop. I was the fund manager of our business so the safekeeping and deployment of the fourth portion was my responsibility. The cash collection was growing gradually and that was very heartening. We were looking forward to making good profits soon. Our spirits were soaring high with the rising profits from our business. Our business had picked up in no time. Many customers frequented our shop daily for having snacks for lunch so we decided to include a meal to our menu. *Chole chawal* was the next addition to our menu and it became an instant hit. We were out of stock within an hour of opening the shop on the day of the launch of our *chole chawal* menu so we had to make huge quantities of *chole chawal* the next morning. *Chole chawal* were selling with jet speed and also helped in selling other snacks which customers bought while waiting to be served. We were getting out of stock soon so we had to keep cooking throughout the day. Our first batch of *chole chawal* would sell out within two hours. We had to keep making more and more as customers were increasing and so was their demand for *chole chawal*. Some customers even got the meals packed to take home as dinner for their families. We could sense that selling meals was a more profitable business than running the snack shop. We had to plan to add more meals to the menu and gradually reduce the snacks. We had to even work on the expenses for the meals to decide on the best combinations for maximum profits. *Rajma chawal* and *curry chawal* were the next additions to our menu. We then included *idli sambhar* and *vada sambhar* and later vegetable burgers to the meal menu. All our meals were a grand success and this motivated us to start cooking early morning at four and be ready with snacks and meals before the customers started to walk in. Customers usually started to stroll in at eight in the morning for snacks and from eleven onwards for our meals. We were not having leftovers and that helped in regulating our profits else it would have added to the expenditure. Twelve noon to three in the afternoon was the busiest slot of the day when customers surrounded our van like bees from a broken hive. It was difficult to keep track of the orders as customers shouted their preferences together. We tried to serve them on first come first served basis but there were still many customers who wanted an out of turn preference. It was difficult to get them to stand in a queue as they were all famished and in a state of hunger that made them incapable of standing in a line. We had to serve the customers at supersonic speed to avoid having the van crowded. Tea was in demand throughout the day. We were looking for an assistant who could help in serving tea and chopping vegetables and another one for washing the utensils as our work had expanded to a level where Mani, Naval and I could not manage it alone. Naval found two boys Jaggi and Deepu who were ready to work for us. He had seen their work at the restaurant where he had worked in the past. He was impressed with their work and got them to join our shop. He and Mani trained them and we were able to get a few minutes of relaxation during the day. Jaggi and Deepu were very young and enthusiastic about their job too and that made them perfect to be part of our business. God was kind and helpful in sending the right people to us for help. He was helping us in every possible way and we felt chosen to have His help. My dream was materializing as desired but I did not want to get contented and stop with the success of *Chutney Haat*. I had to think big and take the business to a higher level and this required more thought and planning.

"What next? How do we expand the business?" were some of the questions that kept bothering me constantly. I was not able to sleep well as I had to find the answers to my questions. I had to fly high and higher. I was desperate to spread my wings and take off into the majestic blue skies. I had to build a house soon so that I could ask Anita for her hand in marriage. And a house looked difficult with this small business setup. I had to think bigger and beyond this business. I felt time was running out even though our business was running well. I had to bridge the gap between this business and my next big move to be with Anita who was standing beyond the bridge.

Business was running well and our profits were increasing. Things were moving well till the day God decided to change the venue of our shop. I was lost in my thoughts when Deepu came running to me. He was in a state of panic and seemed to be startled by something. "Did you meet a vampire on your way Deepu or did you come face to face with a ghost?" I spoke to him jokingly. "They are going to dig the road, this whole place will be dug up soon, we will be thrown out of here, they have come, they are coming towards us, they will throw us out of here," Deepu managed to tell me in a frantic and breathless tone. "We will be thrown out of this place, where will go? What about our shop?" he said in a worried and tensed voice. He was trembling with the fear of the unknown. "Don't panic Deepu, let us not react without finding out what the issue is," I told Deepu as I walked towards Mani. Mani was trying to gauge what was happening across the road. There were signs of some activity in the offing. "Let us go and check what is happening there Mani," I told Mani. Mani and I looked around and saw some people across the road. They were carrying some equipment with them. They set up their equipment on the side of the road and started to measure the road. We went up to them and asked them what they were doing. The news was not good and we looked at each other with questioning eyes as we did not have clear answers with us. We waited to talk to their leader. It took a long time for their leader to get free and give us a chance to speak to him. A bulldozer made a grand appearance with its giant size on the road in front of our shop. Some trucks followed the bulldozer after some time. Then a road roller rumbled in and parked itself royally on the side of the road. We learnt that the road in front of our shop was undergoing some developmental activities. There were people measuring the road and marking it for digging. The parking lot was being extended and redesigned and that meant our shop would need to be moved elsewhere. We had to look for an alternate space soon. Deepu and Jaggi were in a state of panic as though the skies were going to come down crashing on us. I tried to calm them down as best as I could. Mani and Naval did their bit in toning down their worries but all in vain. "Things are not as bad as you think Deepu and Jaggi. We will be fine and our business will continue as it is. Both of you do not have to worry at all. Mani, Naval and I will see to it that you are not jobless. We will make the business run as usual," I said in a comforting voice to Deepu and Jaggi trying to put them at ease and calm them down. I had seen worst days so this situation did not alarm me at all. I knew we would manage our business with ease. There was neither a dearth of customers nor of spots to set shop in Gaulpur. We woke up the next morning to the tremors from the bulldozer at work. We got up to see three more road rollers parked on our side of the road. We walked around to see if any change had taken place during the night. Things looked the same except the road rollers and bulldozer that were parked around us. Some workers in yellow helmets and blue overalls strolled around the area with shovels. The supervisor walked up to us and informed us that we had to close the shop as it was on Government land and he had orders to run it down. "You will need to clear the area as we will be moving the van out of this site," he said to us authoritatively. "We will start in forty minutes. You can collect your stuff and vacate this place before we tear it down," he continued in his drumbeat like voice. "Is there no chance for this stall to be spared?" Mani asked him. "None, this is Government land and we have orders from the Government. You need to pick up speed and clear up. No excuses! I do not like to wait, come on, hurry up, we have to start immediately, come on guys, clear up the van or we can move it with your stuff if you want us to," he retorted in his drumbeat like tone that was now being released at a much higher octave than before. We cleared the van of all our belongings and stood on a side as we saw our restaurant being towed away by a crane. The hook was put around our van's window like a noose and the crane lifted it up slowly. We sighed in traumatic pain and stood there shattered. It was not just a van but it was our dream, our livelihood and our shelter. Mani, Naval and I stood there in silence sighing with Deepu and Jaggi. Deepu was the most affected by the incident as he was the youngest and had probably faced such a shock for the first time in his life. Jaggi was just a degree better than Deepu as he was not trembling as badly as Deepu but his face had deep marks of pain, stress, worry and confusion. "Wish we could do something to stop this, don't know what, but I really wish we could, it is unfair and just when the ball had started to roll and things were moving in our favour. Wish I could stop this somehow, I feel so helpless, this is making me angry and nervous at the same time," Mani ranted in a rapid pace as he paced the road up and down. "I hope this is just a bad dream and things will be back to normal when I wake up, I hope it is just nothing," said Deepu hoping that his wish comes true. "Oh God, please help us. I will do anything to make them stop. Please help us God. I will work sincerely and keep a fast on every Tuesday God, please help us God," Deepu's prayers were taking time to be heard but he kept praying with his eyes closed and his hands folded in deep faith. We could see how much this van and the job meant to him. It was a disappointing end to something we had started with great enthusiasm. Our prosperity seemed to have been short lived and our excitement had been limited by weeks. We were again on the road within months of leaving the Mehta Mansion. "Looks like it is a bad *nazar*, someone's evil eye has brought us this misfortune," said Naval in a bitter tone. "I want to kill the guy with the evil eye and hang him with the hook of this very crane. Remember to hang an old shoe to ward off all evil the next time we set up shop else these evil eyes will keep causing us trouble." Naval kept grumbling at length to himself. I was waiting for Jaggi to add his comments but he was very quiet. He was so sad that he could not even utter a word. He stood there with the sauce pan in his hand and a worn out look on his face. The pain was making his cheeks shrink as he held his tears in his eyes. I told him things would shape up for the better soon and told him not to worry about this at all. Deepu was holding the tree as a baby monkey clings to his mother. I put my hand on his shoulder and told him to have faith. "Nothing is permanent in life. We need to keep moving on. Look at the brighter side of this situation. We might get a better van or an even better spot for our shop," I whispered in Jaggi's ear. I walked to Deepu and repeated the same in his ear. I kept my feelings within me as I was thinking of the next step. I did not want to analyze the past but prepare for the future. The Government order could not be undone so we had to work on our future now. A temporary set up like a canvas tarpaulin or a van was bound to be taken away from us some day or the other for sure so we had to get a permanent shop which cannot be moved or swayed or shaken or towed. I had seen worse and knew that God has always walked with me to see my dreams come true and I was confident of having His company this time too. I chanted the *Gayatri Mantra* and asked for God's support. Just then a thought struck me with the speed of light and I asked the supervisor if we could have a temporary setup near his shed for snacks and meals for his workers while they worked. He pondered over the idea for a few minutes and agreed and asked the crane driver to stop and park our van near his shed. We thanked him repeatedly and he told us it was only a temporary approval. We would need to move out as soon as his work was finished. Deepu and Jaggi were jumping around as they saw the van being parked near the shed. Their faces lit up with abundance of joy that wiped out all their pain and worries in an instant. They had forgotten about the incident in a few minutes in their childlike innocence. Deepu's prayers had been answered and my prayers had been heard too. I thanked God for His help at such a troublesome juncture. He had saved us from being on the road that night. We had been able to get some time to hunt for a new place. Mani, Naval and I knew this happiness would be short lived but we had been able to buy some time to think about our next move. We quickly started to set up our things in the van again. Deepu and Jaggi ran around and lined up everything back in the van. We were back in business and this time we had double the number of customers, the regular ones and the road workers. The sudden turn of events had been very favourable for us. We were obliging the supervisor with free tea and meals. He loved our chutney and the *chole chawal* meal and a free meal is always tastier so he overate each time. The crisis had made our profits zoom up to a huge figure. This had been a blessing in disguise for us. We had to thank God again for this timely help. He had saved us from being on the road. Deepu and Jaggi were the most relieved and went around serving everyone very cheerfully. I could hear them humming a peppy song from a movie. We were safe for the time being but had to find a solution soon as the van was sure to be towed away once the road was made. Time was running out and we had to come up with some options soon. I spoke at length with Mani and Naval after closing shop. We decided to start looking for a place nearby on the road that ran parallel to this one. This would help in retaining our customers. I knew we would have to move again from there too so I wanted to find a permanent place from where there was no fear of being thrown or turned out by anyone. I wanted a place which would be our own. "Don't you think we need a permanent place for our shop?" I asked Mani and Naval. "We cannot keep moving from one spot to the other. We need to get a place that we can call ours." "How do we get a place of our own?" Mani questioned me while Naval looked at me and nodded to seek a response from me. "I will let you know tomorrow? But I think we have to start working on those lines so that we do not run around from one place to the other like vagabonds," I said to them while my thoughts were running elsewhere. "Is this the end of my dream?" I pondered. "How do I go beyond this point?" We required a huge chunk of funds to take our business to a higher level and we did not possess such financial strength to back our business. "Should I ask Mrs. Mehta for help?" I questioned myself. "How will I pay back the money, I need a huge sum and it would take me years to return it," I thought. "I think I have an answer but am not sure about it. Give me a day and I will let you know," I said to Mani and Naval and found them lost in their thoughts too. I walked around for some time and returned to Mani and Naval and told them that we will borrow money and rent a shop where we will set up our restaurant. "But who will lend to us? We do not have anything to mortgage but ourselves, who can possibly lend to us?" asked Mani. "Yes, who will lend to us? And why would anyone lend to us? What is our credibility that anyone in this world would lend to us?" Naval concurred with Mani. "I know someone who just might. Let me speak to that person and I will let you know soon if we are indeed fortunate to get financial help or not," I responded as they looked at me with doubts written on their confused faces. Mani and Naval seemed to think that I was doing some wishful thinking so they did not bother to argue with me any further. Deepu and Jaggi slept peacefully while Mani, Naval and I found it difficult to sleep that night. We spoke about the possibilities and options where we could start our shop afresh but did not make much headway. Naval dozed off after an hour and Mani followed suit and started to snore loudly as his huge stomach moved up and down with his breathing like a dolphin dancing in the ocean. I tried my best but could not sleep at all that night. I was restless and tossing in bed as I could not decide whether to ask Mrs. Mehta for help or not. I was unsure of how she would react to my request. I had finally made up my mind at 3 a.m. and got up and was ready by 3:20 a.m. but had to wait till the sun came up before I could go to meet Mrs. Mehta. I sat outside our van and kept thinking how I would ask her for the help. I was at Mehta Mansion at 7 a.m. that morning. Mrs. Mehta was sitting in her garden. Joy and Polly were rolled up near her feet. They started wagging their tails on seeing me. I walked up to her. "It is so nice to see you Suraj, it has been long, what brings you here Suraj?" she said cheerfully. Joy squealed in delight while Polly continued to wag its tail vigorously. The grass was well mowed and I saw a new gardener watering the plants. I was reminded of the good old days when Lakhan went around the garden with a hose. I wondered where he was as we had not seen him since we left Mehta Mansion. I hoped he must be doing well as he was exceptionally good at his work. I was not sure whether Aditya was home or not. It would have been difficult to speak to Mrs. Mehta in case Aditya was home. I looked around to see if there were any signs of his presence but could not find his car in the porch or the driveway or anything else that might confirm to me that he was at the Mansion.

Chapter 26

"Good Morning Ma'am," I said to Mrs. Mehta. "What have you been doing all this time and did you find a girl or not?" she asked. I narrated to her the story of my life since the time I left the Mansion. She kept listening intently and nodded and smiled occasionally. "You seem to have done a lot in this short period of time Suraj. I am happy to know Mani and Naval are with you. I did get to know about your business some days back and was happy to learn about it," she said. "Ma'am I am here to seek your help," I said wondering how she had got to know about our business. "Yes Suraj, please let me know how can I help you?" said Mrs. Mehta. I told her I needed funds and she was nodding. I was unsure of how she would react but it was a respite when she asked me to come inside the Mansion. She asked me to wait in the main hall while she went inside. I was waiting in the hall when I saw Anita come in. She was surprised to see me. "How are you Suraj and are you here to meet Ma'am?" she asked. "Yes, I am here to meet her," I said. "How have you been?" I asked her as she fidgeted. "I am fine. I believe you have a good business now. I had met Naval some days back in the market and he told me about the three of you and your tea stall," she said. "I am happy to know you are all into a business partnership now," she continued talking to me bringing a smile on my face. "And I informed Mrs. Mehta also and she was very excited to hear about it." "So it was Anita who told Mrs. Mehta about our tea stall. Mystery solved," I spoke to myself. Anita stood there talking to me for a few minutes and then left for Mrs. Mehta's room. It was always refreshing to meet Anita. Things always worked well the day I would see her. She had a sweet smile on her face as she turned around to look at me as she walked towards Mrs. Mehta's room and she nodded at me and again said bye before she disappeared into the house. A little later Mrs. Mehta came out with a big paper bag in her hand. "This is a little more than what you wanted but you may need it so I have brought it for you," she handed over the money to me as she spoke. "Thank you Ma'am, thank you so much. You do not know how much this means to me. I cannot thank you enough for this help. It is God sent Ma'am," I said. My eyes were fixed at the door in a hope to see Anita again. "Is she not a nice little young lady?" Mrs. Mehta commented on noticing my gaze that was still fixed at the door. I was startled by her comment. I did not realize that she had noticed that my eyes had been following Anita. "Who . . . . Ma'am?" I fumbled as I spoke to her. Mrs. Mehta smiled and said, "You know who I am talking about Suraj. She is really good and you should not leave her. Believe me, she is really an angel. Don't let her go away, Suraj," Mrs. Mehta urged earnestly. "She is the girl for you Suraj, believe me, she is just right for you," Mrs. Mehta said in an assertive voice stressing on each and every word that she said. I nodded with a smile, "Yes Ma'am, I will not leave her." Mrs. Mehta smiled and nodded adding her consent to my decision. I suddenly remembered the purpose of my visit to the Mehta Mansion and withdrew my attention from the door to look at Mrs. Mehta. "I will return this to you as soon as I can Ma'am," I told her. "Never mind, she said. It was not going to be used anyways. You will put it to some good use. Do not worry," she said. "But Ma'am I will return it," I repeated myself. "Do not worry Suraj. You can return it when you have it, there is no hurry and there is no need, so you should not worry about it. Just go and see your dreams materialize, make a life for yourself," she said as she smiled at me. "Do you know Aditya means the Sun and your name Suraj also means the same. Aditya and Suraj are synonyms but in real life you and Aditya are so much different in your nature. I like you because you are 'Suraj'," she said with a spark in her eyes. The spark reminded me of my mother who had a similar spark in her eyes whenever we met. I smiled and thanked her again and returned.

$\mathcal{C}$hapter 27

We took a small shop on rent and turned it into a restaurant. We named it *Chutney Haat* again. We worked on the place from scratch and were amazed at the results. We were living in the restaurant as we did not have anywhere else to go. We painted it ourselves. We gave it the theme of clouds in the morning sky so everything had a white and blue combination. The walls were blue and white stripes and the ceiling had a white shade like the clouds lining the morning blue skies. We bought wrought iron tables and chairs from an antique dealer. The flooring was of beige tiles. We selected the lights to match the walls. The lamp shades had hues of the deep blue of the night sky. Our chinaware and cutlery were also in shades of blue. The table linen was blue and white checks with matching table napkins. We got blue and white striped upholstery for the seats for the chairs. The curtains were white and the valences were blue and white stripes. We got blue vases and blue glass candle holders for the tables. We managed a good deal from a shop that was going out of business. This shop had almost everything that we needed and we were fortunate to learn about it just before it closed down and we got majority of our furniture and linen from this shop. The reception and cash counters were wooden tables with blue table linen spread royally on them. The kitchen was open and faced the tables. We could seat twelve people at a time. Our efforts were well rewarded as customers appreciated the ambience of our restaurant. We wanted to have a grand opening celebration party for our restaurant. We personally went to Mehta Mansion to invite Mrs. Mehta. She was so happy to see the three of us together after such a long time. I can still remember the day Mani, Naval and I had walked into the Mehta Mansion to meet her. We walked through the driveway reminiscing the time spent at the Mansion. It was a journey through our past that made it look as fresh as new. We started discussing the golden days spent at the Mansion and remembered the memorable moments spent together at the dorm. Mrs. Mehta was sitting in her garden with Anita. They were knitting something when we walked up to them. The garden looked fresh and lively with seasonal flowers enhancing its beauty. Mrs. Mehta was astonished to see the three of us there. Her face immediately lit up on seeing us. We informed her about our restaurant and invited her to the inaugural party. She was extremely delighted to know about our success. I thanked her for her help, "We owe it to you and could not have done it without your help Ma'am. We will return the money to you as soon as we can Ma'am. Thanks so much for the timely help. You have been instrumental in helping us materialize our dreams. Thanks a lot." "Yes Ma'am, your generosity has helped us in achieving this success, our restaurant could not have shaped up without your help," Mani added. "We do owe it to you alone Ma'am, you have been very kind and helped us just when we needed it Ma'am. Thank you so much for all the help," Naval said thanking her as one end of his moustache flew up with the strong breeze that was blowing with all its might. "You don't have to thank me. Thank all the efforts you guys have put in. You have really proved that hard work definitely brings results. I am so happy for the three of you, I feel so proud and happy, wish Mr. Mehta were here to attend this party. It would have made him feel very elated," she said to us in a cheerful voice. I was happy to see Anita with her as this would give me a chance to speak to her. I moved towards Anita to speak to her when Mani, Naval and Mrs. Mehta were busy talking. "You will need to come too else I will not have the party Anita," I told Anita in a whisper that was loud enough only for her to hear. She smiled at me and nodded. She then bent herself towards me and whispered back, "What if I don't come?" I tilted towards her and again whispered to her, "Then I will not have the party". She smiled at me and her eyes sparkled as she spoke to me, "Really, do you mean it?" "Yes, I mean what I say, ... , each and every word of it," I replied. She smiled again and giggled and opened her eyes wide as she said, "I will surely be there. I don't want you to cancel your party for me!" "I will be waiting for you," I told her before leaving and that brought another smile on her face. Her twinkling eyes had a deep smile and many questions in them as she said bye to me.

The three of us were busy running around arranging for the party. We had to get pamphlet inserts for distribution with the local newspapers. Then there were banners to be made and displayed at strategic locations. We had to decorate our restaurant with ribbons, streamers, lights and flowers. We got our cooks to make snacks for the guests who would come for the opening celebration. It required a long planning for the inauguration. We packed boxes of sweet *ladoos* for the guests to carry with them when they return. Each box had six *ladoos* which we had arranged from a sweet shop. The boxes had stickers of our logo with our address and phone numbers. Yes, the three of us owned mobile phones by then. We were not dependent on phone booths to be in touch with each other and with our families. We also put up banners near the BPOs where we had our tea stall and snack shop to attract our old customers to our new restaurant. We asked the *pandit* from a temple close by to do a *havan* at our restaurant. The *pandit* gave us a long list of things that were needed for the *puja*. Naval and I got them the evening before the inauguration. The *havan* was performed in the morning. Naval, Mani, Deepu, Jaggi and I sat for the *puja*. We prayed for the success of our business and also for our well being. We prayed for our new business to be successful and grow by leaps and bounds and multiply our revenues. We also prayed for the health of our families. The *havan* was over in an hour's time. We packed the *havan kund* and cleared the hall of the *puja* mats and started to arrange the hall for the opening. We set the snacks on the tables together with colas and juices for the guests. Mrs. Mehta was the guest of honour at the inaugural celebration of our restaurant. Anita was the special guest who made me feel overjoyed by her presence at the occasion. I took her on a tour of our restaurant and showed her every little thing around. She was impressed at the effort made by us in every little detail in setting up the restaurant. I was feeling proud of myself as I walked around with Anita. She was amazed at the layout and she liked the blue and white theme a lot. She kept appreciating everything that she saw and that made me feel very happy. She was very chirpy that day unlike her normal reserved self. She was visibly happy with our success. We got about one hundred guests on our opening and were hopeful of having them as our permanent customers at our restaurant. These guests came from the nearby localities. We saw some old customers from the BPO too and that was very heartening and encouraging as we were sure to have them as our permanent customers now. We had arranged for a live band to play at the opening of the restaurant. It was not a reputed band but they were good and created a very welcome feel for the customers. They played a nice welcome tune whenever any guest entered the restaurant. We served lemonade to the guests as they walked into our restaurant. They were then guided to the snacks which were spread on the tables encouraging customers to indulge in them. Our guests ate heartily and we kept churning a constant supply of snacks till each and every guest felt satiated. We wanted them to eat as much as they could and become addicted to our snacks and return to our restaurant for more. Luck was special for us and stood constantly on our side making our restaurant business a grand success. Our efforts did not go in vain as our popularity soared with each passing day. Each day was busier than the previous one increasing our cash flow generously. We had customers in waiting list as the restaurant was always totally packed with guests. I do not remember a single instance when any table was vacant during the lunch and dinner time. It was difficult to manage the customers who were waiting for their turn. We had to put some chairs outside the main door for the customers to sit while they waited for their turn.

$\mathscr{C}$hapter 28

Things were moving just as we had desired and that
made us not just happy but at peace too. We were at peace
but not relaxed as we wanted to maintain our business at
the level where we had reached and we also had to take
it much higher from here. *Chutney Haat* had become a
very popular hangout place for the young crowd. It had
shaped into a fast food restaurant that served the Indian,
Mughlai, Chinese, Italian and Continental cuisines, all
tweaked to the local taste. We had Wi-Fi, good music and
a play area for children in one corner of the restaurant.
The restaurant saw a huge foot fall of customers who
belonged to all age groups. Our Chinese cuisine had
become very popular. Naval was using some unique
recipes to keep the customers wanting more and more.
We had hired six cooks and Naval kept them on their
toes as he blasted them with instructions throughout the
day. He had trained the staff very well as he had the best
experience in serving guests after having worked for a
long time at Mehta Mansion. Jaggi and Deepu were busy
running errands round the clock. There were two cleaners
whose job was to keep the restaurant spotlessly clean. We
were open from nine in the morning to eleven at night.
We were making additions and modifications to our
menu regularly with our growing popularity. We had to

meet the expectations of our customers and that kept us totally engrossed in our business. We hired a Manager to supervise the restaurant and the kitchen supplies. We were in big business!!

We opened the next restaurant close to the railway station. It was my tribute to the platform that had helped me sustain in my initial days at Gaulpur. I offered Sundar the job of the chef at this restaurant and he happily accepted it. Sundar gelled into the business just as expected and was able to manage the restaurant with expertise. The footfall here was unmanageable in the initial days as we were not expecting such a large number of customers to visit us. The passengers in transit found the restaurant cleaner than the nearby roadside *dhabas* which made us more popular with them. The *dhaba* owners took this seriously and tried to poach our staff. We had to find ways to retain our staff as they were really good at their work. Mani and I spoke at length to find a solution for this issue but we always hit a road block. We were in a dilemma as our action could create enmity between the staff of the two restaurants if we increased the salary of the staff here. We called the staff one by one to know what their decision would be. We were sure about their loyalty but money is surely a big incentive. It was a tough situation and we were not able to accept the fact that our staff would leave us for someone else. We did not want to lose our staff as they were really good at their work and we had spent a lot of time in training them. We had not faced this situation till now so it came as a severe blow to us. People had been very sincere and loyal to us till then and we were not prepared to see our staff leave us. We had probably assumed that they would be working with us forever. Our assumption was under question as we gradually came to terms with the fact that they will eventually move on. We had desires to grow and so did they. We could not blame anyone for wanting to prosper but the incident did shake us up. We thought of taking Sundar's views on this and met him. We asked him how he felt about the situation. To our surprise, he was not disturbed at all. He said "Let them go if they want to. I am sure they will return when the *dhaba* owners make them work round the clock and scream at them for the slightest mistake. They will not be able to survive there for long. And even if they do, we can get more staff with ease. Don't worry there are very nice workers at the platform stalls whom we can hire. They will be loyal and not easily tempted. Plus we have a lot of people in Gaulpur to fill in for them. Nobody is ever indispensable at all." That gave us some assurance and we decided to let things move ahead and waited for our staff to unfold their decision. "Sundar was able to solve our problem in a second Mani," I said to Mani, "Now I am wondering why we were so worried about this situation that was not as bad as we had thought it to be." "Yes, I felt the same way after talking to him. He did calm down my nerves. He is a mature person and his thought process is crystal clear," Mani agreed. "We should not expect our staff to continue with us forever. We should be prepared to let them go as they need to grow and find better avenues too. I think we will have to live with this truth and face it now," I told Mani as we returned to our restaurant. "They too have desires like us and we should let them take off and meet their dreams," I continued as we entered our restaurant. We spoke to Naval about our new found perspective. He too agreed with our point of view. We now knew that we had to keep interviewing a lot of people as we would regularly need to hire new workers with the old ones leaving us for other jobs. Sundar helped me change my perception about life in a few minutes. He had given me a new outlook towards seeing things in life. He had dissipated all our worries so gently that it was just amazing. He made a crisis seem of no importance at all and that made me happy to have a friend like him. He had shown me that being calm in a crisis can help solve any problem with ease. I also realized that nothing is too big to worry about in life. I learnt to put myself in others' shoes and see the world from their perspective. I had matured with every experience in my life and this one made me grow as a person and as an individual.

There are times when life itself makes wonderful changes for you and leads you to believe that you have done something really good to deserve what you desire. It was one of such wonderful days a few weeks after our second restaurant had become operational. It led me to an avenue that was to open more doors towards success for us. I have a vivid memory of the day I went to meet Raja one evening at NextEdge. Things changed for the better that day as life opened some more doors for us.

*C*hapter 29

I was waiting for Raja outside NextEdge when I saw a person move out of his office with a dozen tiffin boxes slung on his arm. He loaded them on to a bike and went inside to get another batch of tiffin boxes. He then made another run till he had collected almost forty such tiffin boxes and loaded them on his bike. I was curious on seeing this so I walked up to his bike and asked him what he was doing. I learnt that he worked with a catering firm that supplied lunch to office goers. The firm employed other men like him who delivered lunch boxes on daily basis to staff at various offices. They had to make two trips, one to drop the lunch boxes in the afternoon and another one to collect the empty boxes in the evening. I asked him the menu for the lunch and the cost per box. I interviewed him at length till I had got all the information that I wanted about catering business. I was intrigued by this line of business. I could expand my business and include catering as a new line of service to it. I had to speak to Mani and Naval and find out if they were interested in including this line of business to our restaurant business or not. I asked Raja if he had tried the packed lunch. "It is not like the food one gets from home. At times it is cold and there are times when they forget to cook it fully. And of course sometimes it is too overcooked and mushy and one has to gulp it leaving one's teeth unused. The staff here is not too happy with this caterer. People are looking for a new caterer. This catering firm is very average but I have heard that there are many other caterers who provide very good food," he informed me. I had to act soon and try to grab this golden opportunity that seemed to be like a low hanging fruit which even Babu could reach with his short height. I came back running to Mani and Naval and explained the incident in detail to them. They liked the idea but were not sure if we could manage this easily. "We would need more staff, cooks and delivery boys and a bigger kitchen to manage that kind of workload. What if the office staff decides not to pay us for the lunch? We could end up in losses," Mani put forth his thoughts in a convincing manner. He was right but we had to take this risk. I tried to reason with Mani and Naval. They were seeing my point of view but had valid reasons to be apprehensive. "Let us try with a small setup for just a small number of staff of NextEdge. We can try to get Raja's help in making us talk to the staff there. We just need to get an entry and then our food will speak for itself. It is a great opportunity. They are not happy with the present caterer and we have a bright chance to fill in as the staff is looking for some new firm to supply lunch. We should not miss out on this one as it is God sent. We may not get such a golden chance again," I tried to reason with them as best as I could. We discussed the business in detail and I was able to convince them that we could manage this additional work and we were soon planning to start a catering firm that would supply lunch to office goers. Mani and Naval were not totally convinced but they played along with me. There was apprehension in their minds about the result but they supported me whole heartedly. I had to make this business succeed for Mani and Naval. I did not want them to regret for the support they had provided me. I was nervous but I had to keep my faith alive as I wanted to pull this through. I had to find similar success like our restaurant business in this new catering business too. It would be challenging but meeting challenges had become a habit for us by then. "Should we call it 'HomeFood'?" I asked Mani and Naval. They suggested some more names like '*Ghar Ka Khana*', '*Dhaba Daal*', '*Dabba*' Food, '*Khanadham*' and '*Lajawab*'. We were debating to finalize the name of our catering service when we heard a sweet voice say "I think HomeFood is the best option."

We turned around to see Anita standing at the door. I was overwhelmed to see her. I almost ran towards her but realized we were not alone and stopped. I thought I must again be day dreaming but I was not. I was sure that it was not a dream when Mani and Naval also greeted her. I had a broad smile pinned on my face. Mani and Naval were staring at us questioningly. Anita repeated herself, "I think HomeFood sounds good, it is closer to the heart and of course it will sound like people are having home cooked meals." Mani, Naval and I concurred with a big nod spontaneously. So the lady won and we had finally christened our new Catering Services Business as 'HomeFood'. I was happy and surprised to see Anita at our office. She said she was curious to know how our business was shaping up so she had decided to pay us a visit. The four of us chatted for some time. I could not take my eyes off Anita and she seemed to notice this and smiled at me. Mani and Naval had to leave for some work and that gave me a chance to speak to Anita. I could not ask her much as she wanted to go home but I did manage to drop her at her apartment with a promise from her that she would meet me soon. I told her I wanted to speak to her at length and she nodded. "Yes, I know, I will drop by at your office sometime this week and we can go out for lunch. We will go to your restaurant . . . . and I will pay for the lunch," she said. "No, you will not pay for the lunch, I will," I told her authoritatively. We kept arguing about who would pay for the lunch and I had to finally give in. She was stubborn and assertive. She wanted to contribute to my business and this was one of the ways she had decided to do so. I agreed as I respected her gesture and thoughtfulness. She was a good soul with a golden heart and that is what made her so special. I asked her about Mrs. Mehta. "Ma'am is fine, getting older and Aditya comes off and on. But Ma'am is trying to make the best of life". I was happy to hear about her. "Yes, I wish she has a long life. I have great admiration for Ma'am. She is a very noble and gentle person with a golden heart," I replied. Anita nodded and smiled. "Ma'am has never treated me like a servant. She has always taken good care of me like one would do for one's own child. She is very giving and very humble and noble and of course too kind, her gentleness flows in her actions," Anita expressed her views about Mrs. Mehta with tears in her eyes. Her tears showed her deep love and respect for Mrs. Mehta. This was the first time I heard Anita talk and express herself freely. I listened to her intently as she spoke about herself and introduced me to her childhood and her life. We were getting to know each other better. We had a good lunch the next day and then such lunches became frequent but I did not let her pay from the second lunch onwards. We had a lot in common. Our likes and dislikes, our opinions, our habits, our passions, our views about life and expectations were all very similar. We had turned into the best of friends in a short span of time. Life was cheerful and lovely with Anita being around and part of it. She made life very worthy just by her magnificent presence. My smile broadened whenever I heard her speak. I could listen to her for hours with the same interest. I wanted to listen to her talk forever and this thought enhanced my focus on my business so that I could build a home for her. Our catering business was another step in that direction.

It was challenging to run the catering business as we had to deliver the food ourselves and have cooking done on a very large scale. HomeFood needed a big kitchen and a large fleet of cooks and delivery staff. We set up this firm close to our restaurant to have a greater control on both businesses. It was a tough task to find good cooks. Hiring the delivery staff was also a mammoth exercise in itself as we wanted to hire boys who could drive a bike. Deepu and Jaggi helped find the delivery staff. They had a number of friends and these friends had friends so it was a huge network to choose from. I was reminded of the days when I was looking for a job. I had come far from that situation and was hiring others to run my business today. God had indeed been gracious!! I was thankful for His support and blessings that had empowered me to be able to set up a business. It was a fortunate turn of events that had me blessed to be able to help others. Our catering business picked up with fits and starts. We first started to deliver the lunch boxes to forty of the one hundred and six staff of the NextEdge BPO where Raja worked. We later delivered the *dabba* meals to the staff at some nearby shops also. The staff of NextEdge appreciated the quality of food and also found it affordable. The business picked up gradually as more and more people from NextEdge started to buy our *dabba* meals. We had bought double the number of tiffin boxes required by us so that our boys did not have to make two trips in a day but just one for delivering the lunch boxes and they collected the empty boxes from the previous day in the same trip. This reduced the diesel expense of the motorbikes which made us price our lunch boxes a little lower than the other caterers. I again contacted Raja to see if he would be interested in helping us manage the catering business but he was not ready to take up the challenge. He wanted a comfortable job with least bit of responsibility and stress. I tried to convince him to agree as I wanted someone I could trust to manage this business for us but he was too adamant and did not yield. "You know I am not the person for this type of business Suraj. You know me so well and still you keep on asking me. Do you want your business to fail?" Raja said declining my offer. Then I thought about asking Anita if she would like to manage this business with us. I had seen her interest in the setup and she often had great ideas that seemed to be very innovative. I went to ask her if she would like to join us. It was a beautiful morning when I set out to meet Anita. Life brightened up whenever I saw Anita and the winds started playing a violin while the trees swayed in a chorus. I wanted to ask her if she could join our catering business. She was not at the Mehta Mansion so I decided to wait for her. A servant saw me marching around so he asked me if I wanted to meet Mrs. Mehta. "No, I am here to meet Anita," I said. He told me that she had left with Mrs. Mehta and will take time to return. I had decided I was going to wait for her so I paced the porch up and down with my eyes searching for Aditya. I planned to hide behind a pillar in case I happened to see him at the Mansion. The lack of any unusual activity and the serene silence in the air confirmed that Aditya was not in town. I had to wait for more than an hour before a car drove into the porch. I was delighted to see Anita and Mrs. Mehta come out of the car. Anita smiled as she saw me standing there. Mrs. Mehta was also very surprised. She immediately guessed that I was waiting for Anita. "I will go inside while you two chit chat," Mrs. Mehta said to me as she moved towards the main door to the Mansion.

Anita and I stood there for a few minutes, each of us expecting the other to start the conversation. Anita looked surprised to see me at the Mansion. I broke the silence and told her the purpose of my visit while she fidgeted from one foot to the other. The expressions on her face kept changing as she heard my proposal. Surprise gave way to a smile and then a fear of the unknown and lastly a confused state of mind reflected on her face. Her eyes seemed to be saying yes to everything that I had said but her mind was stopping her from accepting my proposal. She was as hesitant as anyone reacting to a marriage proposal. I had not asked her for her hand in marriage but her reaction seemed to be as though I had popped the question to her. She was nervous and her eyes had too many questions in them. I found it difficult to look into her eyes as they melted me. She was probably expecting me to propose to her but I had put forth a different proposal. She seemed disappointed when she did not hear the right question and her eyes said it all. She smiled with difficulty trying to hide her feelings before letting me know her decision. "Oh, I would love to but I need to take care of Ma'am. I don't want to leave her all by herself. She has always cared for me and now I do not want to leave her when she needs me the most. I am really happy and feel so honoured that you felt that I had the potential to take up such a big business but I do not think I can take it up. And I feel I should not as I have a moral responsibility towards Ma'am. I don't want to leave her. I am really sorry for not being able to take up this job. I hope you will understand Suraj," Anita explained her concerns very apologetically to me. "You could speak to Mrs. Mehta. She will surely agree. Won't you be leaving her when you get married?" I asked Anita as I tried to search for an answer in her deep brown eyes that were trying to say a lot to me. I could see myself in her eyes and that was a special feeling. I was living in her eyes at that moment and she kept staring at me in an effort to capture me and also that moment in her eyes. It was a very significant and special moment as we stood there enchanted and drowned in love. It was a heavenly feeling to be able to understand her without speaking any words. I was thinking whether Anita too could understand me or not. A few minutes later Anita came back to reality and spoke to me, bringing me back from cloud nine to the porch with a thud. "There is time for my marriage and I will decide when the time comes. But as of now I do not think I should leave her. She has done a lot for me. I will be with her till I possibly can," Anita declared her decision with conviction while her eyes questioned me as to why I had not proposed to her. Her eyes were screaming at me to ask her but I kept quite. I looked into her eyes with all the answers in my gaze and could see her reading them before she turned away to look at the garden. She was trying to control her tears and her disappointment. "Anita, don't, please . . . don't cry", I pleaded. I just could not bear the sight of her crying. She looked at me again with her questioning eyes. "I will come back soon with all the answers," I said in an attempt to reassure her as I left. She kept looking at my eyes and said, "I know that Suraj, but when?" She almost whispered trying to stop herself from choking. I could not bear to see her in that state. There was so much pain and anguish on her face as she had patiently waited to hear from me and I had been restraining myself as I could not have given her a good and comfortable life then. I was sorry and could feel her pain and felt worse for having caused her the pain. I wished things could get better soon. I could see that she loved me and she had not tried to hide any feelings from me that day. Her question had cleared any doubts that might have been there in my mind about how she felt about me. I wanted to calm her but did not know what to say to her. She just stood there leaning against the wall and looking at the fountain in the porch. I knew she was angry with me. I tried to say something but could not. I waited for a few moments before speaking to her. "Don't send me like this. You are making it difficult for me to leave. You know I will be back very soon, just let me find a place to stay before I speak to you," I said to her as I looked at her. She looked at me and I could tell by her expression that she was happy to know that I would be back. She smiled softly and nodded as she understood my apprehension. Her smile broadened gradually as she grew confident about my feelings for her. Some birds started to chirp and Joy barked at them drawing our attention to the garden. I turned to look at Anita and I nodded to let her know I meant what I said. She moved her head slightly as she looked at me and wiped her tears. I was sad and felt helpless leaving her there but I had no choice. I had to wait till I had my own place to stay. It was difficult to leave from there with Anita's voice resounding in the porch and the questions in her eyes echoing through the silence of the serene air. I wanted to reply to all her questions and I would do that when the right time came. I had to live with the restlessness for now. I smiled and said bye to her and returned to my friends. I knew her eyes were glued to me as I walked back through the driveway to the main gate. I was disturbed at leaving her there with so many unanswered questions. But I knew I would be answering all her questions soon. I could not sleep that night knowing that Anita must be awake too.

I spoke to Mani and Naval about hiring a new business manager for the catering business. We all had our apprehension on getting someone new. We decided to split the work between us and agreed that Mani would handle the catering business and Naval and I, the restaurant business. Naval teased Mani as he slapped his paunch lightly, "Hope you don't spend the day tasting the food from the *dabbas* and add more fat to your paunch Mani. Just manage with the aroma of the food and leave the food for our customers. I am sure you will put on a few more kilos just by sniffing around." Mani was used to hearing jokes about his obesity so we rarely got a reaction from him when we teased him on that subject. So all we got was a slight smirk on the left side of his right cheek that disappeared as fast as it had made an appearance. Mani readily agreed to manage the business and he was a very good choice for managing this business as we soon realized. Mani was hands on with the business and ensured the quality of food and punctuality of delivery staff. The business picked up slowly and it took us a few months to make headway in this line of business. Then came a time when people from various offices started contacting us for the *dabba* meals for their staff. Our reputation was building up and so was our business. Mani was growing homesick so we decided to send him to Alsi for ten days.

Those ten days were an ordeal as we had to manage the restaurant and catering businesses without Mani's help. We realized how much work Mani was shouldering all by himself. We found it impossible to keep in line with the schedule for the *dabbas* but we managed it somehow though with great difficulty. We got some respite on his return as he came back in high spirits after spending time with his family. He returned with renewed vigour and made the business grow three times within a month. This made us realize the importance of holidays and we decided to ask our staff to take two days off every six months in rotation. This made them come back with substantial increase in their energy and enthusiasm which made them add volumes to our business. The break from work was a boon to our business as we saw our business pick up each time a staff returned and it also kept the staff happy as this was a paid holiday. This even helped us retain our staff as other restaurant owners did not believe in giving any holiday to their workers and they also deducted wages for such leaves taken by their staff. Naval and I were focused on the restaurant business while Mani managed the catering business. I had thoughts of splitting the business amongst the three of us equally to have greater control on our share of businesses. I was feeling guilty of taking the profit share from Mani's business even though I was not helping him in any way. I mentioned this to Mani and Naval who took it to heart. I realized how attached they were to me and the business. Mani would have benefitted the most as we were not contributing to his business but still sharing his profits but he did not want to split. I tried to reason with him but he did not want to listen to any of my arguments. He was happy the way things were running and did not want them to change even if it meant a larger share of profits for him. "We are in profits because we are together. It is our name and goodwill that sells Suraj, how can we split? I will lose half of my customers if I decide to split. Our customers come to us because we have a name and we have created that name together and together we shall stay, and that is final," Mani put forth his argument to us adamantly. "What about you Naval? What do you suggest we should do? I was only trying to be fair to all but Mani wants things to remain as they are. So what is your suggestion? What should we do? What is your decision about this whole thing? Should we continue taking a share from Mani's business even though we are not contributing to it now?" I asked Naval. Naval was indifferent to the idea. He did not mind splitting or staying together and left the decision to us. "I am ok with anything. Suraj, you have a genuine logic and Mani, you have a strong valid point and I am with you whatever decision you take. We will anyways be together whether we split or not. We started this with nothing and struggled together to build these businesses. We stayed together while we struggled so it makes sense to be together when we are reaping the benefits of our struggle." So we decided to keep the partnership in all our businesses even though we were managing separate portions of it. I was happy to have such good friends in this century of the shrewd and cunning when each one is for oneself and even real brothers do not stick together. I was really lucky to have Mani and Naval with me. God had been really very kind in choosing my friends for me.

Chapter 30

I felt sorry for having antagonized Mani but I had to put forth my views to him so that he did not feel that he was being taken for granted. I was glad that I had brought this up even though it had caused some stress between us but I felt at peace with myself after hearing them speak about our partnership and knowing how they felt about our relationship. Life progressed well and smiled seeing the three of us managing our businesses with total commitment. We had good savings by now and all three of us had opened our bank accounts. We were sharing a one room kitchen accommodation at Golden Meadows located about a mile from our shop. This apartment was a lot better than our dorm. Mani and Naval were sleeping in the bedroom and I slept in the living room. We had bought the basic furniture for our apartment. We chose the utensils for the kitchen from a wholesale shop. We had a very basic and modest infrastructure to support us at the apartment. We now had a decent place to live. We could spread and stretch ourselves on our beds and did not need to crouch under the canvas tarpaulin. I could stretch my arms without hitting Mani when I woke up. The walls of the van were no more there to restrict our movement. There was no worry of being disturbed by rains or thunderstorms. We did not even have worries about our restaurant being towed away. It was a peaceful life at the apartment. We finally had a home of our own! But I had to wait to propose to Anita as I wanted an independent home for myself where Ma, Papa, Anita and I would be living 'happily ever after'.

We had come a long way from where we had started. I had moved from Murli with a small bag and two thousand rupees and two sets of clothes and stayed at the railway platform before moving to the dormitory at Mehta Mansion and then I was on the road again when I slept in the godown at the construction site and then under my canvas tarpaulin at the tea stall and then in the van and later at the restaurant before coming to this apartment. I had been through ups and downs and still did not lose hope at any stage. My parents and grandparents had included me in their prayers and blessed me every day. Mani and Naval had been with me through thick and thin. I was very fortunate and privileged to have them around. Mani's wife and children supported him emotionally by agreeing to his decision of moving back to Gaulpur. Deepu, Jaggi and Sundar had also been very supportive. And of course I had the initial guidance and motivation from Babu who was instrumental in sowing the seed for our business. Then it was Mrs. Mehta who helped us financially to see that our small sapling matures into a fruit bearing tree. And Raja had disappointed me each time I had asked him to join our businesses. Anita was the reason for every decision that I took to progress in my business. Above all it was God who had made all this happen. I would keep thanking God for His immense help. I knew God was walking with me through my dreams to see that they get fulfilled. God had been kind and helpful throughout my journey in Gaulpur. I had come a long way with His help. I could look back and trace the journey of my life with great pride.

Chapter 31

Our restaurant chain had increased to nine outlets in the city within five years of its launch. We were known to have the largest billboard in every street. *Chutney Haat* was now called 'Chutney Sauce'. Business was flourishing just as I and Mani and Naval had dreamt. We were planning to expand our operations to other cities also. Chutney Sauce was a well known name now. We had started home delivery service through a call centre. We asked Babu to join us as the Catering Manager for the home delivery business and he agreed. We had various people working for us to manage our staff and our accounts and funds. We advertised through radio where the famous radio jockey Mrs. Tasleem Khan's jingle for our 'Chutney Sauce' became a well known song that youngsters liked to hum, "*Chutney Sauce hai aisi kamal, karti hai dhamal,sabke aane ka hamen hai intezar, to aayen janab, karen Chutney Sauce Restaurant mein daawaten hazar.*" Things were moving at a good pace and our business was flourishing and our profits were at their peak. Life could not have got better for us. We were reaping the benefits of our hard work.

My parents had moved in with me after about two years of the launch of Chutney *Haat*. I had taken an apartment on rent and my parents liked to be with me. Evenings were filled with comforting family time. It was great to be with family. Ma and Papa were settling in the Gaulpur culture and lifestyle that was very new and different for them. They liked this new lifestyle where they did not have anything to do. They were far from the fields and livestock. My uncle was managing our livestock back at Murli. He was also in charge of our ancestral house while we were in Gaulpur. We had two servants to help us at home but Ma insisted on being the kitchen queen. She did not let the servants cook. My mother did not want us to eat from our restaurant so she cooked all the meals for us. It was a treat to have delicious meals cooked by my mother after a tiring day at work. Mani and Naval often came home with me to join us for dinner. They loved my mother's cooking. Naval was a great fan of her cooking and that made me very proud as he had never liked anyone else's cooking till now. Life was moving smoothly and I planned to propose to Anita as I could afford to buy a home now. We had both waited patiently for this day and I can never forget the happiness on Anita's face when I proposed to her. She almost let out a cry and started to dance when I asked her. The world had come to a standstill as she circled on her heel and said "Yes" to me. "Yes, yes, yes," Anita said excitedly as she accepted my proposal and jumped up in joy. It was the happiest moment of my life. I then took her home to meet my parents. She was elated to meet Ma and Papa. My parents were also happy that I had made the right choice. Ma hugged us both and blessed us.

I asked Ma to give Anita the green sari. Ma looked at us in surprise and said, "How come you have kept this sari with you till now. I thought you would have given it to Anita when you returned to the Mehta Mansion after Diwali that year when you took up the job at the Mansion."

Anita looked at me all surprised, shocked and confused on hearing that I had the sari for so long. She put her hands up in the air with her mouth open on the revelation as she could not believe what she had just heard. She was astonished at the news. "I cannot believe what I just heard. I am amazed that you took so long to propose to me when you had taken the decision that year," Anita said to me in a state of total shock. "How could you hold on to the sari for so long? You sure have a lot of patience, Suraj. You kept me waiting for so long. I feel like a fool now. Even Ma and Papa knew about it and I was not even aware! All this while I had been thinking that it was only me who had feelings for you and you did not feel the same way for me. I now get to know that you just kept me waiting for no reason at all. What prevented you from proposing to me then? I am so, so, so very disturbed by this that I am not going to speak to you at all." She was very annoyed with me and could not control her anger.

"You know I was trying to make a home for us. I could not have told you anything till I was sure that I could give you a good home," I tried to reason with her but she ignored me and walked out with Ma to the kitchen while Papa chuckled and laughed at the episode. I followed Anita to the kitchen and stood there near the refrigerator for sometime but Anita kept ignoring me. I smiled at her every time she turned to open the refrigerator in an attempt to pacify her anger but she completely ignored me and did not speak to me all through the day. She kept talking to Ma through the afternoon and was silent even when I went to drop her in the evening. She did not look at me even once during the ride to her home. I tried to do everything that could please her but she did not give in till the next day. I was happy to see her wearing the green sari the very next day and knew that she had finally forgiven me. I went to pick her up for lunch at Mehta Mansion and saw her in the green sari. I could not take my eyes off her as she came out to meet me. The sari made her look divine and so beautiful that I could have stood there all my life in admiration of her beauty. The breeze started to hum a song of love as she walked to the car. She had walked into my life like a dream and had swept my sleep away. She looked like an angel with green wings who had flown down from the skies just to meet me. She caught me staring at her and blushed.

"Looks like you are feeling better today," I said to her softly as she glared at me angrily. I could see her eyes twinkling with abundance of love overflowing in them, the love for me, even though she tried to look angry with me. So I tried to tease her. "That looks like a fake expression on your face," I pointed my finger to her face as she tried to look away. "No, it is real and I am still angry with you, very angry, but am trying not to say anything to you because I do not want to spoil my mood," she said pretending to be annoyed with me. She tweaked her lips and looked away. "I don't think so. The sari seems to say that you have forgiven me," I said looking at her from the corner of my eye. I knew I was irritating her with my behaviour but I wanted to make her feel better. I held her hand and said, "Ok, I am sorry, I really am, I did not do anything intentionally. You know that I had just wanted to give you a comfortable life and did not want to commit to you. Imagine how hard it would have been on you if I had given you a commitment and not honoured it?" I tried to make her see things from my perspective as she gave me an indifferent glance. I remembered this glance from the day we were travelling to Dori so I teased her. "You had the same look on your face at Dori too. You should have had faith when the priest tried to unite us! You know our being together was inevitable, we were united by the priest in the temple of God!" I smiled and winked at her. She smiled back and looked at me with a twinkle in her eye. This twinkle spoke volumes of her love for me. I was fortunate to have her in my life. I tried to reciprocate the twinkle with a smile and a loving blink of my eyes. That was a moment of true love!! Love, that was showering its blessings on us!! "I know what you are trying to say. I just wish that you had expressed your feelings openly much earlier than you did. I did get subtle hints from your behaviour but a girl likes to hear it directly from the person she loves, but you decided to keep mum about it. What if I had found someone who had been more open and got married to him? What would you have done then, Suraj? I am sure you would have still waited to build a home!" she made a face at me as she opened her heart by stressing on every word that she spoke. "No, Anita, no, I would have never let that happen. If there had been someone else I would have immediately declared my love to you. I would not have let you leave me, Anita. Please don't misunderstand my intentions. I was just planning for a comfortable life for us. Each time I tried to expand my business, I did it only for you. I always had you in mind each time I took a step forward in life, wish I could let you know what you mean to me. You are my life and my world, Anita. Your thoughts kept me moving ahead each time I felt let down by life or thought of giving up. I could not have come this far if it had not been for you, Anita," I explained to Anita as she looked at me with her twinkling eyes. She nodded and smiled at me. "I know that Suraj, and I also want you to know that you are also the most important person in my life, Suraj, you mean the world to me too," Anita said to me in her sweet voice making me feel on top of the world. I was overwhelmed and found it impossible to contain my happiness on hearing this. I told her I was sorry for what had happened. "I promise you that I will keep in mind that things are clear and open between us from now onwards. I will try that we do not have any differences that make you so . . . . , indifferent . . . , towards me." Anita smiled on hearing this and again made a face at me. "I do not like it when you ignore me. It is hard for me when you become so quiet and make me feel unwanted and disliked, and I just fall apart on seeing your pretence of being angry with me when you have actually forgiven me," I continued. "Ok . . . , I also promise not to ignore you but you need to be more open and honest about everything," she responded with a smirk. "Love you," I responded with a blink of my eyes as she smiled lovingly at me with that special twinkle in her eyes. I kept staring at her waiting for a response but she decided to tease me by keeping me waiting. Her mischievous smile gave her away as she stopped as soon as she started to speak. She looked away while I waited for her to say something. "I think we should move now, Ma and Papa must be waiting for us Suraj," and that was her cold response to my "Love you." I concealed my disappointment at not getting any response from her and nodded and started the car and we drove home. We were lost in ourselves as I turned the steering wheel of my car. The car moved smoothly gliding on the road as it too was in love. Our love had grown infectious and it spread across. The weather too was beautiful and totally in love. It was a short drive home as we were not living too far from the Mehta Mansion. We smiled at each other and walked into our home where Ma and Papa greeted us. They had invited Mani and Naval for lunch too. Anita nudged me and nodded telling me to break the news to Mani and Naval. So Anita and I broke the news of our engagement to Mani and Naval who were very happy for us.

Anita surprised me as she whispered, "Love you too," in my ear. I looked at her and smiled again as the sparkles in her eyes looked like a starry night sky with stars shining brightly all over her. I could have hugged her but restrained myself. Her words were like the sweet notes overflowing from the strings of a violin that plucked the strings of my heart. The love between us was divine that made us feel content. There was love wrapped all around us and we were all smiles in a heavenly bliss.

"I could tell something was surely cooking between the two of you," Mani managed to talk while he took a bite of a *samosa*. "I am very happy that you are together. So we have a wedding in the family soon. And lots of good foo . . . . d, I just can't wait for the wedding and all that food at the reception. I want to be in charge of the food at the wedding." Mani garbled as he kept chomping the *samosas*. Naval too smiled and congratulated us and hugged me. "Great to hear about you both! Wow! Just feel wow! Congratulations Suraj! Congratulations Anita! So when is the wedding?" "It should happen soon, I want to enjoy the food," Mani immediately responded making us all split into laughter. "Is that all you can think about Mani?" Naval asked. "And you are just in the right business too," he joked while Mani's eyes surveyed the snacks on the table. Mani was in love with food and his eyes were just stuck on the table. His life began and ended with food. He could immerse himself in a barrel of food and stay inside contented all his life as long as the barrel was topped up with food. He was lucky to be in a business that gave him ample opportunity to always be with the love of his life . . . . food!

Mani and Naval were visibly happy for us. They picked me up in their joy and started to dance. Ma could not help laughing at us as the three of us danced. Papa called us all to the living room and addressed Mani and Naval. "We invited you to plan and fix the date of the wedding; after all you are both part of our family." Mani and Naval nodded and sat down as Papa started his speech. He had a long speech that described all his plans and expectations about the wedding arrangements. We went into a long discussion and planned the wedding while Ma cooked a lovely meal for us and Anita and Naval laid the table. Mani gorged himself with food while the rest of us discussed the wedding. Anita and I were in a different world altogether knowing that the wedding would be taking place very soon. Our dreams were coming true. We kept exchanging glances as the wedding was being planned by our family. I kept nodding for every suggestion put forward by Ma, Papa and Naval without even listening to them as I was lost in Anita's eyes. Mani spoke twice in the entire discussion as his mouth was full for the rest of the time. Anita also nodded when Ma spoke to her as she too could not take her eyes off me. We were so lost in each other that we did not feel the presence of others in the room. We were seated opposite each other and spent the entire afternoon gazing into each other's eyes with the humdrum of the conversation of Ma, Papa and Naval and the munching and chomping sounds from Mani serving as the orchestra in the background. It was a very dreamy and mystifying afternoon where Anita and I were together and alone in the world in spite of being surrounded by our family. Anita could not stop smiling as her joy was immense to be easily contained. I was happy not just for me but also to see her so happy. The sun shone from the window on the dining table giving Anita's eyes a hazel touch and her hair a golden hue making my dreams appear painted in gold. She looked like an angel with her captivating beauty. She had flown down directly from the heavens only to fulfill my dreams. I could not have asked for more from God. I made her blush each time I looked into her eyes and my heart missed a beat every time she blushed. We were lost in our own world while our family planned our wedding.

Anita joined us for lunch every day and stayed with us till late evening. Mrs. Mehta had given her the permission to be away from the Mansion. She knew that we needed this time together. Ma and Anita spent hours shopping for the wedding. Ma had informed Nana and Nani about the wedding. Their joy knew no bounds. They reached Gaulpur as soon as they learnt about the wedding. Nani immediately grew fond of Anita. Our home was filled with happiness and so was our life. Nana and Nani were overjoyed as they helped in all the preparations for the wedding. Mani and Naval obediently listened to all their instructions and helped in making the arrangements with total perfection. They were very excited about our wedding and wanted to make the celebrations memorable by making the best possible arrangements.

An year later I bought a palatial house near Mehta Mansion. I named it 'Ashirwad' as it was possible for me to own this villa only with the help and blessings of Mrs. Mehta and it was my way of showing gratitude to her for her help. It was indeed her blessing, her *ashirwad,* that had made this a reality and I was indebted to her for life.

Naval and Mani also bought Villas near Golden Meadows. Our homes were within five kilometer radius from each other. Mani was able to convince his parents and wife and children to move to Gaulpur. Naval was planning to marry and settle down. We were all settled and in heavenly bliss with everything falling in place for all of us. Life was perfection personified for us. I was delighted to see the happiness on my parents' faces when they entered 'Ashirwad'. They were overwhelmed to see the guards open the gate for us as we drove into our own Villa. It reminded me of the first time I had entered Mehta Mansion. I had a Villa of my own now. I was delighted as my dream was getting fulfilled as I was not driving but had been driven in a sedan by a driver in white uniform to my very own Mansion. My parents took pride in living in Ashirwad Villa. It was definitely my dream house. Ashirwad Villa was our gateway to a new lifestyle of grandeur and prosperity. I invited Mrs. Mehta for the house warming function. She was delighted to see our new home. She had tears in her eyes when I told her why I named it *Ashirwad.* She was touched and I just could not stop thanking her for helping me reach where I had. I had to thank Mrs. Mehta for the initial financial help that had made us come so far. I returned the money she had lent me as I dropped her home. She was surprised to see the packet in my hand. She was not expecting me to return the money to her. "There was no need to return this to me Suraj, you should not have," she said to me as I handed the packet to her. "I had told you not to return this, did'nt I," she said. "But I had to Ma'am. It was very kind of you to help me when I needed the money. Our life has totally changed just because you helped us at that time. Ma'am you cannot imagine the number of people you have helped with this money. It is not Mani, Naval, me and our families but also our staff and their families who have a comfortable life today because of your help. I am returning it as I can afford to return it now. I have taken a long time to return this money to you Ma'am but I could not have kept it with me. I also have to thank you and Mehta Sir for the job at your Mansion. It was only because of this job that I could meet Anita, the love of my life," I said to her as she took the packet from me. "You gave me my first job in Gaulpur and you gave me Anita who has filled my life with so much happiness and brought brightness into my life. I owe a lot to you Ma'am. I shall forever be grateful to you." "I just tried to help you Suraj, that's all. I am glad that you put the money to right use," she said in her sweet voice. I thanked her again and returned home thinking about how many people had benefitted by her help.

The prophecy of the priest at Dori had come true, I was married to Anita by then and yes, I did invite Mrs. Mehta to our grand wedding!! My Nani had made the wedding dress for Anita. My parents and Nana and Nani were the proudest hosts at our wedding. Mani and Naval handled all the preparations at our wedding like my real brothers. It was a wedding to remember! They had put their soul in every little detail at our wedding. Mrs. Mehta blessed us and was very happy to be invited to the wedding. "Did'nt I tell you Suraj that you will make it big one day," she said. "And I also told you Anita is just the girl for you," she winked at me and smiled.

I smiled and looked at Anita who smiled back at me and God stood there with us like He always does!!